THE BOOKER

A SAM QUINTON MYSTERY

THE
BOOKER

A SAM QUINTON MYSTERY

KEVIN R. DOYLE

CAVEL
PRESS
Kenmore, WA

CAMEL PRESS

A Camel Press book published by Epicenter Press

Epicenter Press
6524 NE 181st St.
Suite 2
Kenmore, WA 98028

For more information go to:
www.Camelpress.com
www.Coffeetownpress.com
www.Epicenterpress.com
www.kevindoylefiction.com

Cover design by Scott Book
Design by Melissa Vail Coffman

The Booker

Library of Congress Control Number: 2024952662

ISBN: 978-1-68492-324-3 (Trade Paper)
ISBN: 978-1-68492-325-0 (eBook)

For Tina O, who's been there for so much of the journey.

CHAPTER ONE

ONE MONDAY MORNING IN LATE SEPTEMBER, sweat beaded on my forehead as I attempted to do a move that Keri Eckland, my assistant manager, had described as a flower opening upside down, or something along those lines. I could think of a whole lot of things more fun to do than embarrassing myself in The Blaster, the gym I've owned for some years now.

I don't care much what the current terminology is. The Blaster is a gym. Not a workout center, not a spa, not a wellness place. Times may be changing, but I grew up in gyms, meaning my place is a gym, pure and simple.

Other things are not quite as pure and simple, at least not to me.

After a couple of weeks of what she called negotiating, and I considered badgering, Keri had talked me into setting up a small section in the back part of the gym as a yoga space.

Keri's a native of St. Louis but has lived in Providence, Missouri, for several years now, and she recently finished up her degree at one of the local universities. A slight woman with blonde hair and blue eyes. While I call her the gym's assistant manager, with only two employees, the title may not mean a whole lot. Then again, how many vice presidents does your average bank have?

She finished her degree in nursing and once or twice had mentioned wanting to work in geriatrics. Despite how much nurses are in demand these days, for some reason she's decided to hang around and work for me a little bit longer.

Only a few weeks after suggesting we add yoga to the gym, her proposal began to pay off. We started out as one class a week and had expanded to three a week, and we were considering moving up to one a day.

All well and good, until Keri had another brainstorm and managed somehow to convince me to join one of the classes.

"It'll be good for business, Sam," she explained the day before with Lisa Nolan, the actual manager of the gym, nodding her red hair in agreement. "When they see the owner of the place taking part as much as anyone else, think of the reaction we'll get."

The reaction I could imagine getting was a lot of young to middle-aged limber women laughing as a man cruising closer and closer to the fifty-year mark tried to keep up with them.

When you have only two employees, though, and they're efficient enough that without them you'd probably end up in receivership, you go along when you can.

There I was, taking part in my first yoga class, convinced the creaking of my joints was managing to mask all the titters coming from the other participants. There were other people on the mats hovering around their fifth decade, but they were all female and, as I studied them covertly, a lot better maintained than I was.

I also couldn't actually see anyone smirking at my discomfort, which could only mean they were all experts at concealing their mirth.

I could only imagine the conversation that would go on over various cocktails later in the day.

As I did my best to follow Keri's instructions, I figured I was seconds away from collapsing in a pretzeled heap on the mat. Right about the time I had begun huffing and puffing, a man in a lavender silk blazer walked in and started looking around.

I didn't see him at first, of course, as my tortured breathing was taking all my attention. It was only when, to my eternal gratitude, Lisa Nolan yelled out to me from the front desk that I knew salvation was close at hand.

"Sam," she called, "guy here to see you."

I somehow lowered myself to my knees, paused to use a small hand towel to wipe the sweat from my face and, staggering to my feet, ignored Keri's scowl as I threaded my way through the other participants and off of the mat.

I had no doubt Keri suspected I had arranged for Lisa to come call on me barely fifteen minutes into the session. Regardless, the visitor gave me all the excuse I needed to get the heck out of Keri's range of sight before I snapped a ligament or two.

As I walked up to him, standing patiently at our registration counter, I looked the guy over.

He was of medium height, medium weight and medium complexion. He had brown hair cut a bit too long to be stylish, at least for the Midwest, and brown eyes behind gold-framed sunglasses. The glasses had red lenses, which also didn't seem very Midwestern, and I'd hate to think about how much his jacket had cost.

Besides the blazer, he was wearing tan slacks, black mesh shoes, and a black shirt opened at the throat. He appeared to have missed a couple of days shaving.

A very definite, almost visible, air of new money as he was showing off his wealth by how he dressed—and this new money missed some good taste as it floated around him. I found myself hoping mightily he was a client.

"Mr. Quinton?" he asked as he held out his hand.

"That's me," I said as I shook it in return.

"My name's John Carson."

"Yes?"

"I'm here to make you a business proposition."

"You mean you want to hire me?" As we spoke Lisa, who stood behind the counter, did her best to appear focused on her computer screen.

I had a hunch what was going through her head. This guy didn't fit the bill for a regular client of the gym, and he looked way too above the class of client I usually get for my side gig.

"No," Carson said, "not hire you as such."

"Sorry, Mr. Carson," I said, "but I don't need any insurance."

Carson grinned, as if I'd made some kind of a joke. "From what I hear of you, Mr. Quinton, you need more insurance than most people. But that's not why I'm here."

"Oh?" By this point, Lisa wasn't even trying to appear like she wasn't listening in.

"Oh is right," Carson said. "I'm not here to hire you or sell you anything."

"Then what exactly do you want?" I asked.

The small grin on the man's face exploded into a full-out smile as he reached into his pocket, pulled out a pale blue business card, and handed it to me. "I want to make you a star," he said.

CHAPTER TWO

"**M**AKE ME A STAR HOW?" I asked a couple of minutes later. John Carson and I had moved to my office in the back of the gym. When we walked in, he looked all around, swiveling his head back and forth. Then his shoulders deflated a bit.

"Is this it?" he asked.

"Is it what?"

"Is this where you do your work?"

I walked over and sat behind my desk, looking again at the business card he'd given me out front. It identified him as John T. Carson, TV Producer, and gave the name of a production company I'd never heard of.

"You get many jokes about your name?" I asked. "Seeing as you work in television?"

He gave me a blank look. "No," he said. "Why would I?"

I shrugged and gestured him to one of the client chairs in front of my desk. He gave one more look around, then shook his head and sat down.

Almost as soon as he sat, he glanced over my head and behind me, and I knew what he was looking at.

"Monumental Productions?" I said.

Carson beamed. "That's right."

"I don't know much about show business, Mr. Carson, but isn't there a possibility of someone confusing you with Paramount studios?"

"Possibility? It's what we hoped for when we chose the name."

Obviously, I knew even less about show biz than I thought. "So what's a Monumental Productions?" I asked.

Carson pointed at the wall behind me. "That's your championship belt, right?"

"It is."

"You were a big-time pro wrestler, correct?"

The guy obviously preferred asking questions to answering them. "Not all that big," I said. "I was only in a major promotion for about six months."

Carson frowned. "But you were a champ, right?"

I debated seeing how hard I could flick his card back at him. "I was champion in the small leagues, not the big time. And being champion only means the promotion's owner likes you a lot and thinks you can make money for him. It's really not that big of a deal, but what do you think I can do for you, Mr. Carson?"

He finally leveled his gaze on me. "Monumental Productions is a studio."

"I pretty much figured that."

"We mainly package series concepts for the major streaming services."

I had a weird notion where this was going and again considered flicking the card his way, maybe putting a little English on it as I did so. "Netflix?" I asked.

"Uhm, we haven't quite cracked that market yet."

"Amazon Prime?"

"We're working at starting negotiations there."

"Disney?" I said, about at the end of my knowledge of modern TV production.

Carson shook his head, though he seemed to regret doing so. "They handle most of their stuff in house."

"Any shows I may have heard of?" I asked.

"Sure," Carson said. "You ever see *Two for Tango*?"

I shook my head.

"How about *Three for a Party*?"

Another shake on my part.

"Maybe *Sexy Sixes*?"

I shook my head again. It was starting to get monotonous.

"Okay." Carson canted his head a bit. "Actually, we're still look-ing for our first really big hit."

"And your studio's been in business how long?" I asked.

"About eight years, but we've got some really good financial backing."

"Must have," I said, "but what's all of that got to do with me?"

Carson grinned, and I suddenly felt like a mouse that had stepped into a trap. He raised his hand up to me, shaped like kids do to show a gun, and cocked his trigger thumb.

"Are you kidding?" he asked. "It's got everything to do with you. The Blond Bomber? Once a professional wrestling champion and now a big-time private eye? You're gold, baby, and we're going to make you the next big thing."

Baby?

CHAPTER THREE

Twenty minutes later, John Carson and I were still in my office, both of us with a cup of fresh coffee.

"So you want to do some kind of show about me?" I asked.

He nodded "Yeah. One of our interns is from this area. She was back home last year and heard some stuff about you on the news. Some murder case involving a politician?"

"Something like that," I said.

"And you were helping out the cops because they were stumped and couldn't break the case?"

"No," I said, "not like that at all."

"Really?" A slight trace of confusion appeared in his expression.

"How 'bout we say you're understanding of that case last year is a little off," I said.

He shook his head and rolled his eyes. I don't think I've ever seen anyone do both of those motions at the same time. "Doesn't matter. It still sounds good. We had our intern do some digging on you."

"Yeah?"

"For sure." He nodded his head a tad too vigorously. "It's a great story. Former national wrestling champion turned PI. The market will eat it up."

"I wasn't a national champ," I said. "Only a local champion."

Carson frowned, as if I'd started speaking in Chinese. "But you worked for the big boys, right?"

"For half a year before I blew my knee out."

"Doesn't matter. Wendy can find a way to smooth that out."

"Wendy?" I asked.

"Wendy Truell."

"And who is Wendy Truell?" I asked.

"Sorry. Wendy's my partner and co-producer."

"You thinking of some kind of reality series?" I asked.

Carson took a swig of coffee and beamed at me. "Of course, we are. You're on your own, running around solving crimes that stump the police? How many ways do I have to tell you this'll be a gold mine."

"Like all those previous shows you mentioned earlier?" I asked.

Carson drank some more, swallowed, then shook his head. "No, those all weren't quite as successful as we'd hoped. Mainly because we were copying other people's templates. This one will be our own original, and it's golden."

I felt a tension in my shoulders and worked a bit to loosen them. "And what if I don't want to go along with it?" I asked.

Carson peered at me as if I was something he'd discovered crawling up his leg. "Not go along with it?"

"Yeah," I said. "What if I don't want to have anything to do with your show?"

"You don't want to be on TV?" he asked, his face scrunching with mild confusion.

"Not particularly."

If anything, his eyes narrowed even more. "But don't you want to make a lot of money?"

"I've got a fair amount now," I said. "Enough to get me most of what I need or want."

Carson shook his head. "I can't believe this. Are you sure? Everyone wants to be on TV."

"Look, Mr. Carson. I'm not saying no. I just don't want you to assume I'll jump at anything without looking it over. What exactly is the idea you have in mind?"

Carson sat a little straighter. His world had realigned itself a bit. "It's a doozy of an idea. Wendy and I came up with it together.

What we do is assign a crew to you, and they follow around and record your activities as you go about solving a big case. We'll have the footage spliced with some interview clips with you as you explain the behind-the-scenes stuff."

He sat back in his chair, smiling as if he'd won an Emmy for Best High Chief Ruckamacka.

"And?" I asked.

"And what?"

"And what do you do if things are as they are now, where I don't have a case to work on?"

His eyes flickered. "You're not working on anything?"

I shook my head. "'Only my end-of-the year membership review for The Blaster."

"Got any prospective cases coming up?"

"Not as far as I know."

"So what were you planning on doing today after you got done with that yoga stuff I saw you doing?"

"Probably some paperwork. Maybe clean up around the gym a bit. Catch up on my reading."

"Reading?" he said

"Yep."

Carson closed his eyes and hummed a bit. At first, I was concerned before I realized he was probably trying to find his inner Zen, or something like that.

You never know what guys who wear lavender blazers are thinking.

I thought about his offer for a minute. While I couldn't quite see myself running around with my daily life surrounded by cameras, as I'd told him I didn't have anything else going on today and wouldn't exactly be wasting my time by listening to more of what he and his partner had to say.

But I also thought about the good old days, in my youth, where I was kind of a local star for a while. I remembered the lights, the audiences cheering for me, and all the good times at the end of the night's matches, when the other boys and I would hit downtown St. Louis for fun and games.

Those days were well in the past, yet it was possible I was being offered, if not a return to the old days, maybe something that came kind of close.

Besides, if I got on TV in any way, shape, or form, Lisa Nolan would love it and promote the hell out of it for business.

In the end, though, it was my lack of anything else scheduled at the moment that decided me to say what the hall and give the guy a chance.

"Tell you what," I said, "why don't we talk more about this."

Carson stood up and offered his hand. "You won't regret it, Blondie. Wendy's back at the hotel. Why don't we go there and have a long talk?"

I wondered if it was only my imagination that made the producer's hand feel slightly oily. If he did it again, I'd have to make it clear I only allow certain people to call me Blondie.

CHAPTER FOUR

THE FIRST POTENTIAL SPEEDBUMP ON MY road to superstardom came as soon as Carson and I stepped outside of The Blaster and into the parking lot.

"Can we take your vehicle?" Carson asked. "I'd like to get a feel for how you move around your town."

I wasn't sure what he meant by that but decided if I pushed it he'd probably explain. "Sure," I said, "right over here."

I started walking towards my car but noticed after four steps Carson wasn't with me.

I turned back. "What's wrong?"

"What's that?" he asked, pointing past me.

I looked in the direction he pointed, then turned back to him. "It's a Jeep Cherokee, cashmere pearl color. Why?"

Carson shook his head back and forth a couple of times. "No, that's not right. Not right at all. A guy like you needs to drive something with some fire. You know, like a Ferrari or a Lamborghini."

"You ever drive a Lamborghini in rush hour traffic?" I asked.

"Maybe we should take my vehicle instead," Carson said as he turned a quarter ways and pointed towards a sky-blue Corvette, complete with rental barcode sticker, about forty feet away.

"Mr. Carson," I said, "I'm not even sure I can fit into something like that."

"When we begin filming, that won't be a problem. We'll have the body and roof modified on whatever ride we pick for you, and it'll look great. I hear they did the same thing for Tom Selleck back on that old TV show of his. You know, the one set in Hawaii? You think a guy that tall could actually fit into a Ferrari?"

At the moment I didn't care less about old TV stars and their cars, and I was already beginning to weary of John Carson, superstar producer.

"This is what I drive," I said, gesturing towards the Cherokee. "You want to go meet your partner or not?"

After a little more grumbling, Carson climbed into the passenger seat of the Cherokee.

"How old is this thing anyway?" Carson asked.

"About six years."

He craned his head to look my way. "You drive a six-year-old car?"

"Sure. What about it?"

"But it's not even a classic. What do the babes say when you try to pick them up in it?"

"I'm a bit past the picking up stage," I said through partially gritted teeth. "And at the moment there's only one woman in the picture."

Carson nodded, reminding me of a plastic bobble head. "Is she a woman who hired you to save her from the mob?"

"Huh?"

"You know, she was married to some rich guy, who actually was a shill for the mob."

"Listen," I tried to interrupt.

"Then he gets knocked off, and the gangsters frame her for it, and you had to dive in and set everything right."

"No," I said, putting as much emphasis as I could into the one word. "She's an administrator at one of our universities. And she wouldn't know a mobster if one walked up and bit her."

Carson harrumphed a bit but settled into his seat.

"Where we going?" I asked.

"Wendy and I are staying at the Trithorn. We were told it's the best hotel in the area."

"Probably so," I said, "though I haven't been in there for a while."

"How come?"

"Last time I was there, a few years back, I had a run-in with some gunmen."

Carson leaned toward me as far as his seat belt would allow. "Really?"

"Look, Carson," I said as I pulled out of the parking lot and onto Arena Avenue. "Don't get the idea my life is like one never-ending James Bond movie."

"That's okay. What do you think producers are for? Wendy and I have already worked out how to smooth over some of the snags in your story."

"Snags?" I asked as I turned left onto Main Street. The Trithorn was about ten minutes away, depending on traffic, and I suddenly wasn't sure I could tolerate my passenger that long.

"Yeah," he said. "For instance, this town."

"What about it?"

"Well, no offense guy," Carson did a dramatic swiveling of his head as we headed down Main Street, "but it's not exactly the most exotic place imaginable."

"You expected exotic in Missouri?" I asked.

Carson grinned. "We'll take what we can get, of course. But we were kinda thinking of having you relocate. Don't you have some sort of touristy lake around these parts?"

I'd just pulled up to a red light, which allowed me to turn and stare at him. "Come again?"

The producer held up his hands, palms out. "Don't get me wrong. It won't be permanent or anything. Only while we're filming the show. We figure it would be good local color."

"Are you talking about the Lake of the Ozarks?" I asked.

Carson actually snapped his fingers at me. "Yeah, that's the one."

"But that's not where I live and work," I pointed out as reasonably as I could.

"Well, duh. But with a few tweaks, it would make for awesome TV."

"Tweaks?"

"Yeah, you know. Make sure there aren't any neckbeards in any of the shots."

"Neckbeards?" I said, though I knew what the term meant.

Carson held up his hands, palms out. "Don't get me wrong, guy. I've got nothing against local people, but if we want ratings, when we frame all the shots, it's got to be Gucci all the way."

"You don't see a whole lot of Gucci around the Lake," I pointed out.

"Hey, guy, what do you think production budget is for?"

"Carson," I said, "if driving a Lamborghini in urban traffic would be ridiculous, it'd be downright impossible down at the Lake. Most of the speed limits are no higher than thirty miles an hour."

The light turned, and I shifted my attention back to the road. Another six blocks to go. If I could make it.

"Okay, we'll put that on the backburner for now" Carson said. "Something much more immediate anyway would be your attire."

"My what?" I asked.

"Your clothes. We'd have to spiff you up quite a bit."

"Really?"

"Really. I mean, seriously, jeans and a tee-shirt?"

"I sometimes wear a windbreaker over the tee-shirt," I said.

"I know, but it doesn't really help out."

"Every now and then I put on a polo shirt. I could even round up a lavender one if you wanted me to."

"No worries, big fella. Once the show's greenlit, we'll be able to budget a better wardrobe for you."

Considering I still hadn't agreed to do any sort of show for him, the guy was taking a lot on faith.

We pulled into the parking garage behind the Trithorn, this early in the morning managed to get a reasonably clear and close spot, and exited the Cherokee.

Carson looked around, as if searching for something or someone.

"Anything wrong?" I asked.

"Huh? Oh, no. Just wondering if it's always this cold around here?"

"The temps are in the mid-seventies today," I said. "About right for this time of year. I guess even that's a far cry from L.A. weather though."

"L.A.?"

I gave Carson a look. "I assumed that's where your offices are located."

Now he gave me a kind of sheepish expression, like a little kid caught snatching a candy bar off a convenience store shelf. "Actually, our main offices are in Fresno. But we do a lot of business with the L.A. types."

"Uh huh," I said as we turned and headed into the hotel. I was feeling even less likely to sign any kind of agreement with the man.

Even though it was shaping up to be kind of a unique way to spend the day.

A couple of minutes later saw us getting out of an elevator on the hotel's top floor. We went to a corner room at the end of the hallway. Going by my impression so far of Carson, I wasn't sure what to expect from his partner.

But actually, I got a rather pleasant surprise.

Carson had to knock twice before the door opened, but when it did it was worth the wait. The woman standing there, who I assumed to be Wendy Truell, stood a good five feet eight. She had thick, wavy hair, brown enough it was almost black, that went down to her shoulders. She wore a rust-colored skirt, boots to match, and a white silk blouse. Her face and figure were all anyone could have hoped for.

"This him, John?" she asked in a low, mellow voice.

"Wendy, Sam Quinton, otherwise known as The Blond Bomber. Blondie, Wendy Truell."

I shook Wendy Truell's hand at the same time I inwardly squirmed at Carson's use of my old wrestling moniker. The Blond Bomber had never been a huge star, and as the years between the end of my career and present day got farther and farther apart, fewer and fewer people even knew the name.

There were a few close friends, very few, who I allowed to call me by the old nickname, but I've noticed that the older I get, the more I want those old days to fade away.

"Come on in, Sam," Wendy said as she stepped aside. Carson and I walked into the suite.

Wendy motioned me to the couch while Carson headed straight to a sideboard to mix himself a drink.

A little early in the day, seeing as it was still morning, but I guess to each his own.

"I'm glad you came," she said. "How much has John told you about our plans?"

"Only that you were thinking of doing a reality show about me, and he thought the Providence area wasn't chic enough for it. You aren't thinking of calling it The Blond Bomber are you?"

Carson did half a snort as he finished mixing his drink. He looked at both me and Wendy, and we both shook our heads. Shrugging, he sat down in a light blue easy chair catty cornered from the couch.

"Actually," he said, "that's how I wanted to go. Felt natural and catchy. But Wendy here pointed out it could be confusing. People would get it mixed up with Blond Bombshell and think the show was about Marilyn Monroe or somebody like that."

"And," Wendy said, "our marketing people nixed the idea as well. We're currently working on some new title concepts."

"Should I point out I haven't agreed to any of this yet?" I asked.

Wendy glanced at Carson, who shifted his gaze away from her. "I thought you told me the other day he was a lock," she said. "That he'd already agreed to come on board."

Now it was my turn to look over Carson's way. If he hadn't been a grown man, I'd have said he was squirming in his seat. "Come again?" I asked.

"I didn't say he was a lock, Wendy. Just that things were pretty much set but needed to be shored up a little."

"You mean shored up as in bothering to tell me anything about it?" I asked.

Wendy leaned back and released an exasperated amount of air. "John, is today the first time the two of you have talked?"

"If by talk, you mean spoken face to face," Carson said, "well, yeah."

I was now more than a little amused and sat back myself to see how it played out.

"What about," Wendy said, "if I mean on the phone, or by Zoom, or communicated in any possible way?"

Carson squirmed some more, and I began to really wonder if they were full partners or not. "Okay, Wendy, today was the first I reached out to him. But I wanted to do it in person, you know? Bring on the full razzmatazz."

I wasn't sure if I'd ever in my whole life heard someone legitimately use the phrase razzmatazz.

Wendy Truell turned back to me. "I'm sorry about this, Mr. Quinton. But we really are interested in doing something with your story. I hope our," she flicked a glance over to her partner, "initial injudiciousness hasn't turned you off."

"Depends on exactly what you want and what you're offering," I said.

Wendy smiled, and Carson settled down a little.

"What we're considering," Wendy said, "is an initial run of eight episodes, detailing your day-to-day life and experiences."

"And you think anyone would be interested in that? I'm basically just a guy trying to make a living."

Wendy amped up the smile another kilowatt or so. "Of course. But you've got to admit you're something of an eclectic character. With the right packaging, we think we could make you into a fairly major star."

"Got a lot of experience in making stars?" I asked.

Wendy shot another glare at Carson, who went back to squirming a little. "John has probably told you we're still looking for our first real breakout show, something to put our production company on the map, so to speak."

"And you think I may be it?"

She slumped in her seat and stretched her legs a bit. "We want to do your story."

"And what do I get out of it?" I asked.

"Fame, recognition, fans. More business for your health club."

"It's a gym," I corrected her, "but you haven't yet mentioned anything I can't live without."

"Money?" Wendy said.

"How much are we talking?"

Wendy turned to Carson. He mentioned a figure.

I gawped at the both of them. "That's for eight shows?"

"Eight shows will take, on average, two to three weeks each to produce. Obviously, that's quite a chunk of your time. Then there's the backend."

I felt myself edging up to a pit of Hollywood, or perhaps Fresno, doublespeak. "What's backend?"

"A percentage of the profits," Carson said. "That would be open to negotiation. Plus, a cut of any merch sales, streaming residuals, all the usual."

"I'm feeling at a disadvantage here," I said.

Wendy laughed, stood up and went over to the sideboard to pour herself a cup of coffee. "Do you know a good lawyer? Or maybe we could hook you up with an agent to handle all of this."

"I know a hell of a lawyer, but he specializes in criminal stuff. And wouldn't the people I'm negotiating with securing an agent for me be a conflict of interest?"

Carson frowned, while Wendy turned with her drink in hand and gave me a look. "You're not exactly what I expected, Mr. Quinton. You have something of a grasp on this already."

"Did a lot of dickering for cash back in my wrestling days. You'd be amazed at how often smaller promoters carp about paying you what they promised. Even now, every now and then there's a client who doesn't want to pay his bill."

"Why don't you talk to your attorney friend? Even though this isn't his specialty, surely he can give you some names."

"I may," I said, "but before that, there's a few other things to iron out."

"Such as?" Wendy asked.

"Such as I'm not really working on anything at the moment, at least nothing in the detective line. So what is there to film?"

"You've got no cases going on?" Wendy asked.

I shook my head.

"Not even anything minor? Like bail jumping or divorce work? We could always spice it up."

"Actually," I said, "I tend not to do that sort of thing. Since I have my gym for my main income, I can be a little choosy in terms of the clients I take on."

Wendy frowned at that, but her partner jumped in.

"If necessary," Carson said, "we can do some window-dressing to make it look like you have an exciting case. You know, something where the cops are completely stumped and come to you because you're the only one who can possibly solve it?"

Wendy Truell gave a short snicker and stood up. "Mr. Quinton, do you have any plans for dinner?"

"Yep. Going to meet up with the woman I'm currently seeing."

"Perfect. Would you mind if John and I join you? Maybe by talking to both of you we can make this venture make a little more sense."

I doubted that, but the prospect of these two interacting with Talia Sanderson was enticing as all get out. "Let me make a call," I said.

CHAPTER FIVE

"WHO IS SHE? WHAT'S HER DEAL?"

"John," Wendy Truell murmured.

Carson waved his hand. "I'm only trying to get the story. You say this is your main gal, right?"

"I prefer to think of her as the woman I'm seeing exclusively," I said.

We were seated in Milton's, a locally famed pizza shop down by the university. Almost six on a weekday, students and assorted others packed the place, but I'd managed to snag us a table for four in the far back. Talia had called a couple of minutes ago to explain a faculty meeting had run late but she'd be there soon.

"So exactly what's her story?" Carson asked again. "Is she some hot young number you saved on one of your cases and the two of you have never separated?"

"Not exactly," I said.

"Maybe her deadbeat husband was murdered by the Mafia, and you saved her from the same fate?"

Wendy began to look a little pained.

"Actually," I said, "she's the dean of the social sciences department at the university."

Now it was Carson's turn to look like he hurt. "No," he said, shaking his head. "I don't think that will work. She needs to be a young thing, twenty-something or so, you know, prime of life and all that. After all, we'll be dressing her up in shorts and tight tee-shirts."

"Mr. Carson," I said, trying not to hiss, "I'm not exactly young myself."

"Of course not, but it's okay. You're a guy, after all." At which point, Wendy Truell looked even more put out. "But we're going for the prime demo, you know. The youth demographic, 18-34."

"And what does that have to do with . . ."

"The young women will watch because they'll see you as a father figure," Carson interrupted. "The guys will watch for your hot girlfriend. See? Everyone's happy."

His partner didn't look very happy at the moment, but I was temporarily saved from more argument as Talia walked in the door.

She spotted us and came our way. I stood up and held out her chair, which she took while giving me a smile that made my day.

When I sat back down, I saw Carson looking more confused than ever.

"This is her?" he asked me.

"This is she."

Talia's a little younger than me, but not by much. I personally think she wears her age a lot better than I do. Lately, she's been wearing her blonde hair down to her shoulders with a little uplift at the bottom, and she usually wears clothing to complement her bright green eyes. Today, she had on a navy-blue jacket, grey skirt, and forest green blouse.

As I made introductions, Wendy looked amused and Carson sputtered.

Talia shook hands all around and sat down. I leaned over to give her a quick peck.

Before anyone could say anything else, our server, a young brunette woman with "college freshman" written all over her, came by and distributed water and menus. We thanked her and she moved off.

Three of us opened our menus while Carson stared at Talia. "How'd you two meet?" he asked, a bit bluntly I thought.

If Talia was caught off guard, she didn't show it. Presiding over faculty meetings all year will toughen up anyone.

"Actually, it was on one of Sam's cases," she said.

I silently groaned, and I'm pretty sure Wendy did the same.

Carson nodded, a bit like a bobblehead doll. "Let me guess. A divorce thing? You thought your husband was having an affair and it turned out he was mixed up with shady characters who bumped him off?"

Talia looked at me, arching one eyebrow.

"Carson and Wendy are television producers," I said.

"So you mentioned over the phone. What kind of shows do they make? Have I seen any of them?"

"God, I hope not," I said.

"We mainly do reality shows," Wendy put in, a forced smile on her face.

If Talia's eyebrows had gone up any more, they would have met her hairline. She turned back to Carson. "No, that's not quite what the case was."

Carson nodded, his enthusiasm undampened. I was beginning to think nothing short of a nuclear attack would faze the guy. "Was it that someone stole something valuable from you, maybe something of your dead husband's, and he was the only man you trusted to get it back?"

Talia managed to give me a quick sidelong glance without turning away from Carson. "Where would you get an idea like that?"

"Well," Carson said, "I hope I'm not out of line, but you look like a pretty classy woman. I'm guessing you come from money. Are you maybe a retired jewel thief? You know, and your old gang tried to pressure you into committing one more big score for old time's sake?"

"Mr. Carson . . ." Talia began.

"Wait, I've got it. You work for a college, right?"

"University," Talia corrected him.

"Sure, yeah, a university. And they've got museums and stuff, right. Did a gang of crooks blackmail you to help them set up a heist, and you turned to Blondie to save you?"

"John," I said. "Talia's a dean. The closest thing she could get to stealing would be a box of paperclips."

Carson's mouth dropped open, and Wendy Truell held her napkin up to her mouth, I assumed to cover up a smirk.

Before anything else could be said, the server came by to take our order. Miltons serves pizza by the slice, and all of us went that way. Talia and Wendy also ordered salads. I ordered my standard two slices of pepperoni, but Carson had ordered four of the meat lovers, causing me to yearn for my younger days when my metabolism was more efficient.

After the server left, Carson took it up again.

"Then you're like a teacher?" he asked Talia.

"A dean's a bit more than a teacher, Mr. Carson. Basically, I run one particular college in the university."

Carson's brow furrowed. "So exactly how did you meet up with a local tough like Blondie here?"

I found myself gritting my teeth every time he used my nickname. Much more, and I'd have to go to the dentist for some repair work.

Talia smiled in a warm, reassuring way. "Sam was investigating a case that involved my department."

"A murder?"

Talia looked my way. "Yes," she said, "it was a homicide."

"What happened?"

"John," I said. "I'm not sure it's the kind of thing to talk about over dinner."

Carson frowned for a second, then nodded, and Talia looked up at Wendy. "A reality show about Sam?" she asked.

Wendy nodded. "One of our staff heard about him and gave us the idea. It sounded pretty unique. A former professional wrestler now working as a private detective? The concept alone could be our ticket to the big time."

"And what would Sam get out of it?" Talia asked.

"He'd be paid, of course. We'd come to an agreement on a standard salary during the course of shooting. Plus, since the show would be focused on only one person instead of a gaggle of wannabes, we could probably work out a percentage of the revenue as well."

"Gross or net?" I asked, mainly so I wouldn't continue to sit there and have people talk about me.

Before Wendy could answer, the server came back with a big tray she set up on one of those folding cart things and handed out our food. She asked if we needed anything else at the moment, and after glancing around we all shook our heads.

There were a couple of minutes of bustling around, unwrapping of napkins from utensils, and general settling down. The four of us spent a couple of minutes in beautiful silence munching our food before Wendy spoke up again.

"As far as whether you got a cut of the gross or the net profits," she said, "that would be up to the lawyers to negotiate. Then, of course, if the show's a hit and goes several seasons, the percentage could go up a couple of points each season."

"Plus, the money you'd rake in at your gym from the publicity that would ensue," Carson pointed out.

I glanced at Talia to try to guess how she was taking all this, but she gave me only a straight poker face with maybe a hint of gleam in the eyes.

I decided to prod her a bit. "'Course, the problem is they want to make some changes," I said.

"Changes to what?"

"Changes to me. I should relocate my business down to the Lake and get a different type of car."

"Car?" Talia asked, the gleam replaced by confusion.

"Something sexy," I said. "Like a Maserati or some such."

"Oh God," Wendy said. "John, what have you been talking about?"

Carson grinned. "Wendy's more or less the financial end of things. I'm the high concept guy. But while we're on the topic, a couple of other points to nail down."

"Such as?" I asked.

"What's your relationship with the local cops like?"

"Pretty good," I said. "I've got a few close friends, one in particular, and a lot of the force works out at The Blaster."

Carson's face clouded, and he shook his head a couple of times. "Naw, that won't work at all."

"What do you mean, Mr. Carson?" Talia asked.

"He's got to be a rogue, you know. On the outs with the local force. Having to stay one step ahead of the law while he works his cases."

Wendy got a sick look on her face. "John, for Christ's sake . . ."

"Mr. Carson," Talia interrupted, "I don't think you quite have an understanding of the community here."

"Another thing," Carson said as if she hadn't spoken, "is we've got to change up your base of operations."

"To what?" I asked. "You mean your idea of moving me down to the Lake?"

Carson nodded. "Right, but we also need to put you in a seedy, storefront office where all the riff raff come and go."

"Sure," I said. "A seedy storefront. Lots of those down around the Lake area."

Carson leaned back, now that I'd finally gotten it a satisfied smile on his face.

"So let me get this straight," Talia said. "You want to do Sam's story as a reality show, showing his life and work."

"Uh huh," Carson said.

"But you want to change what he drives, where he's located, his relationship with the police, and what kind of office he has. That right?"

Instead of answering, Carson gave both of us a full-wattage smile while Wendy Truell looked as if she wanted to slink under the table.

"And you call it reality?" Talia asked.

Carson nodded in response.

"One small question," I said. "If part of the appeal of this to me is publicity for my gym, what good does it do if you don't actually show me anywhere around there?"

Carson's smile slipped a couple of notches as Wendy threw up her hands.

CHAPTER SIX

JOSH NICHOLS, DETECTIVE SERGEANT IN THE Providence police force, snickered at me. "A TV show? About you, Blondie?"

Since I've been out of the wrestling game for as long as I have, few people bother to call me Blondie, short for The Blond Bomber, anymore. There's even fewer I tolerate it from, but Nichols was one of those—unlike Carson, who the other day hadn't gotten any of my hints about laying off the name.

It was early the next afternoon. I'd called Josh in the morning and invited him to lunch. We met up about twelve thirty in the downtown location for the Subporium, a small local chain of sandwich shops.

"I'm glad you see the humor in it," I said.

Another snicker. "Come on, Blondie. No offense but doesn't the whole thing sound a little . . ." He waved his hand as he groped for words.

"Whackadoodle?" I supplied.

"Sounds about right. You aren't really talking to these people are you?"

"Never hurts to hear someone out, especially if there's money involved."

Josh nodded as he took a bite of his BLT.

I'd always wondered why The Subporium, as good as their food is, hadn't branched out into at least a regional chain, but whenever I considered it I was kind of glad they hadn't. Although there are few truly local establishments of any kind these days, Providence is lucky enough to be home to several, of which our current location counts as one of the best. Josh had his BLT on wheat, and I had an Italian special with extra dressing, and we were both happy as could be.

"And the fact you asked me to lunch the very next day is coincidence, right?" Nichols asked.

Grinning, I reached into my pocket and pulled out a typewritten sheet. "Here's a quick profile of the two main players."

"Gotten from where?" Nichols asked.

"Off the internet."

"Why are you pushing it across the table to me?"

"Thought you could run the names," I said. "Let me know for sure if they're legit or not."

Nichols hadn't yet picked up the paper. "And how's a small-town cop from the Midwest supposed to get that kind of info? You think I'll just call up California and they'll open the books to me?"

"Not really. But I'm sure someone with your legendary ability as an investigator should be able to slither under a couple of doors."

Shaking his head, Nichols put down his sandwich and picked up the paper. He glanced at it for about a second before looking back up at me. "Are you serious? John Carson? And he works in television?"

"Yeah," I said. "I tried to point out the irony, but it went right over his head. These folks don't exactly talk and think like real live people Josh. At least Carson doesn't. I'm still not sure about his partner. She seems a little more grounded."

"So before you decide whether or not to parade in front of the cameras, you want to know if you're getting a bum deal or not. That it?"

"That's about it."

Nichols shook his head again. "Sounds flaky as all get out to me, but what the hell. Crime's been down in town for the last week or so. I'll make a few phone calls and tap a few buttons. See what I can find out."

"Thanks, buddy."

"I assume if I get called on the carpet for this you'll give me a job?"

"Why not?" I said. "According to my producers, they're going to make me a big star."

CHAPTER SEVEN

B Y NOON THE NEXT DAY, I hadn't heard anything from either John Carson or Wendy Truell. They'd given me their number, but since the whole thing was their proposition, and I had plenty of other work to do around the gym, I figured it better to wait to hear from them.

Truth be told, I wasn't all that sold on the whole idea. I'd had a brief little fling with fame back in my wrestling days, a limited type of fame, and all it had gotten me was a busted-up marriage and having to look for a new career at the tail end of my thirties. I wasn't sure I wanted to go down that road again.

I also hadn't heard back from Josh Nichols, which didn't bother me much. Nichols was first and foremost a civil servant, and I knew he'd get around to my favor when he had the time, but checking out a couple of yo-yo's from California who'd wandered into town would naturally take a back seat to actual police work.

I spent the day in my office doing some paperwork, making a few phone calls to venders, and leafing through the assorted mail that had accumulated in the last few days. I was well aware Lisa Nolan could do all this busywork and then some, and not only wouldn't she have minded, most days she much preferred running everything herself, but I had to do something to feel I was making a contribution beyond my name being on all the official documents, and I had a sneaking suspicion if I didn't, I'd show up one day to find the locks changed.

By mid-afternoon, I'd done about everything I could think of to do and was contemplating calling it a day when my phone rang.

"Blondie," Josh Nichols said as I answered, "it's me."

"Get what I need?" I asked.

A hesitation, slight but noticeable. "Not yet, and it may be academic anyway."

"Meaning what?" I asked.

"Have you heard anything out of Mr. Carson today?"

When a cop answers a question with a question, it's time to sweat a bit.

"No," I said, "but I'm assuming I will sooner or later."

"Maybe not, Sam."

Now definitely time to sweat.

"What's going on Josh?"

"We're here at the Trithorn, and I think you'd better get here. Lieutenant wants to talk to you."

When a detective lieutenant leaves his office and heads into the field, it can only be for a couple of really serious things.

"What's up, buddy? Give me the lowdown."

"It's the Truell woman. She's lying dead in her hotel room."

A natural death of some sort would hardly have caused the detectives to be brought out, leading me to only one possible conclusion.

"Murdered?"

"Looks like it," Nichols said, "and we're really interested in your buddy John Carson."

CHAPTER EIGHT

T HINGS WERE HOPPING OUTSIDE THE TRITHORN hotel. Located on Main Street at the eastern edge of Providence's downtown, one street away from a private college, within spitting distance of an independent pizza shop, and bracketed on the other side by an entire block of downtown shops, there ordinarily wasn't much out-front parking to begin with.

When the hotel had first been conceived some bright architect, city planner, or somebody like that had no doubt taken one look at the area and said "Oh, hell no," in terms of putting a major hotel right smack dab in the middle of all that. The builders had come up with an effective, if pricy, solution to the problem by installing their own parking garage set back a ways from Main.

On ordinary days, their solution worked pretty well.

This didn't seem an ordinary day.

As I drove past, I counted four patrol cars parked on Main, taking up all sorts of lanes and real estate, which made me not even consider heading into the parking garage. Instead, I pulled into the lot of Zippy's Pizza and parked there, about four slots down from an ambulance with three attendants sitting on the bumper, munching away on pizza slices and drinking out of paper soda cups.

A couple of minutes later, I exited the elevator on the fifth floor. A young patrolman, who looked to have some amount of Korean ancestry, barred my way.

"Sgt. Nichols is expecting me," I said.

The cop tilted his head a bit. "You a friend of the sergeant's?" he asked.

I held my hand up in a flat plane and wavered it back and forth.

The patrolman grinned. "May want to step lightly, dude. The lieutenant's in there as well, and from what I hear he ain't too happy."

The cop stepped out of my way, and I headed down to Wendy Truell's room.

Nichols hadn't bothered to give me the room number, and I didn't even need it. The door stood wide open with five uniformed officers standing outside and a small parade of plainclothes folks, detectives, lab techs, and assorted other personnel, parading in and out.

I waited a moment till I had a clear shot, then stepped over the threshold and, noticing the door and frame were intact, looked around for Nichols.

The room was actually a suite, which didn't surprise me. The main room held a couch done up in black leather that could fit four, a 50-inch television bracketed to the wall, a king-sized bed, two floor lamps, and a little inset spot for a dry bar.

I couldn't see what the rest of the suite look liked, but it was obvious upon stepping inside that that wasn't important.

Nichols and Lieutenant Santiago were in the main room of the suite, standing on each side of one end of the leather couch. While the usual crime scene activity swirled around them, Nichols had the worried look on his face he usually did at homicide scenes, while Santiago stood ramrod straight, his arms folded across his chest.

Josh Nichols, in his mid-thirties, looks about as you'd expect a cop to look. He'd started out as a patrolman back in St. Louis, where I'd first met him when he moonlighted doing security for the Midwest Wrestling League. After a few years in uniform there, he'd gravitated back to his hometown of Providence, gotten a job on the force, and before too long had graduated up to plainclothes. He'd made detective sergeant around the time he turned thirty, which said a lot about his work ethic and effectiveness.

Lt. William Santiago's a little younger than me, somewhere in his early forties, with brown wavy hair. He carries himself well and keeps himself in shape. Not native to the area, he arrived in Providence a few years back after spending almost two decades on the Chicago force. There had been a lot of talk back then, and some of it still hung in the air, as to why a man with his level of experience would seemingly take a step down and come to the relative sticks of central Missouri.

The fact he ordinarily dresses in suits that cost as much as the house payments of most people I know helped fuel a lot of the talk.

At five ten, the lieutenant is quite a bit shorter than me, and he weighs a whole lot less. But his lean, muscled build, along with the casual hardness of his expression let you know he wasn't someone to mess with.

I'd only made it three steps inside before they both looked over at the same time. Nichols waved me over.

I'd barely known Wendy Truell, but the timing of our acquaintance didn't matter. It's still a shock to see someone seemingly in the prime of life with a bullet hole in their face.

She had on a silk crimson robe with black piping and, as far as could be told, nothing else. She was slumped with her head resting on the pillow at the end of the couch. Except for the blood and gore around her, she could have stretched out to take a nap.

Far as I could tell, it was a single shot. The front of her face wasn't too messed up, except for the entry wound, with most of the damage apparent from where the slug or slugs exited the back of her head.

A highball glass containing some sort of mixed drink sat on the coffee table next to an open laptop with a blank screen.

The originally green couch pillow was drenched in red.

"Jesus," I said.

"Nichols tells me you knew the woman," Santiago said by way of greeting.

"More like met. I probably spent a grand total of forty-five minutes with her, if that."

Santiago jerked his head, and the three of us walked back out into the hallway and down a ways to talk in private.

"Hotel has her registered as Wendy Truell," Santiago said.

"That's the name I knew her by."

"And Sgt. Nichols here tells me that yesterday you asked him to check her and another person out."

Nichols looked a little sheepish, but Santiago didn't seem to notice.

I figured what the hell, he'd hear it all sooner or later anyway. I laid out the entire story. When I finished, Santiago spent about five seconds shaking his head.

"You think they were serious? A TV show about you?"

"Have you been paying attention to popular culture lately, Lieutenant? They make those shows about everybody from race car drivers to plumbers."

"You sign any paperwork or anything yet?"

"Of course not. All we did was talk a couple of times, and we didn't even get that detailed."

"You don't know anything about any friends or family?" Santiago asked. "Anyone she might have known in the area?"

"You're thinking of the fact she would let whoever it was into her room," I said.

"The fact the door wasn't forced seems to suggest that."

"And if so, plus the fact she's dressed only in a robe . . ."

"Means she probably knew whoever let her in," Santiago finished the thought.

"More than likely," I said.

"Be my guess."

"I'm not an expert," I said, "but to my eyes it looks like an almost point-blank shot."

"Seems that way to us as well, but we'll wait for the experts."

"Exit wound," I said.

Nichols nodded. "Which means there's a slug somewhere in that mess of gunk on the couch."

"If it is point blank, she not only let them in, she let them get really close."

"Like someone she probably really knew," Santiago said.

"Or a pro," I said.

The two cops looked closer at me while the activity of the crime scene people went on around us. From out in the hall, I could hear the murmur of activity.

"Why the hell would a professional killer be taking down a TV executive in Providence, Mo?" Santiago asked.

"Not saying one did, Lieutenant. Just it's a possibility."

Santiago grunted and went back to staring at the deceased woman.

"What does Carson have to say about it?" I asked.

The two cops glanced at each other, and a little tightness formed in my gut.

"Be nice to know," Santiago said, "but so far we can't find him."

"Doesn't he have a room here?" I asked.

"Sure does," Nichols said. "Next floor down. A uniform and I already went down there."

"And?"

"And it looks about like the hotel room of a guy traveling solo for a week or so. Clothes in closet, shaving stuff and toothpaste in the bathroom, damp towels on the rack. Bed pulled back like it's been slept in but not made yet."

"But no John Carson," I said.

"Nope. There's even about a half-eaten breakfast on the coffee table. But your guy's nowhere to be found."

I mulled that one over while Nichols and Santiago gave me their best beady-eyed cop stare. "Anyone at the hotel seen him recently?"

Santiago looked pained. "Get it straight, Quinton. We barely got here ourselves. We're going through the procedure step by step, which means we'll get around to canvassing the rooms before long. As of now, though, your guy seems to be in the wind."

"He's not my guy," I pointed out, "but it seems pretty clear the first thing is to grab her phone and see who she's talked to recently."

"You're right," Santiago said, "and for what it's worth, even without you around we already figured out that would be the way to go. Except we've tossed these rooms upside down, and there's no phone we can find."

"Damn," I said, "that kind of puts a kink in things."

"Can you tell me anything about her," he gestured at the deceased, "that I don't already know?"

"If so, can't imagine what. Like I said, I've barely spoken to the woman."

"Same with this Carson fellow? And is that his name for real?"

"As far as I know," I said, "but the guy's kind of goofy, Lieutenant, and when I called him on it, he didn't seem to know what I was talking about."

We stood around and looked at each other for a few minutes.

"Kind of makes him look guilty, doesn't it," I eventually said.

"It does."

Something popped into my head. "Tell me if you've already thought of this, Lieutenant, but how's he getting around?"

"Meaning?"

"Meaning he's from out of state, way out of state. When I met him the other day he was driving a rented 'Vette. Really light blue in color."

"Yeah," Santiago said. "He registered the car with the hotel when he checked in, and we've got all the units keeping an eye out for it."

"If he's smart, he'll have ditched it," I said.

Santiago cocked his head at me. "But you've already said the guy doesn't seem too bright. I'm hoping he'll be dumb enough to keep driving the rental around. Make it a lot easier to bring him in."

"Assuming he's even anywhere close to still being in the area," I said.

Santiago turned to Nichols. "Anything else yet that's developed?"

Nichols shook his head

Santiago frowned. "We have two people who've come in from out of state to make the acquaintance of the All-American Kid here," he hooked a thumb to me, "and forty-eight hours later, give or take, one winds up murdered, and the other's adrift somewhere. That's what we have, right?"

"That's about it."

"Wonderful." The lieutenant turned his frown on me. "Thanks for coming down, Quinton, but it's time to take a hike now. Keep in touch in case we need you for something."

"Absolutely."

"On the off chance you hear from this Carson, you'll let us know, right?"

"Of course, Lieutenant. Though I can't really imagine his reaching out. If he did this, he's probably halfway home by now."

CHAPTER NINE

"WHAT HAPPENS NOW?" TALIA ASKED ME later that night. We were sitting out on her deck, enjoying takeout Chinese from a restaurant on Main Street. Talia had a white wine and I, after a couple of days of dealing on and off with Hollywood people and having one of them die on me, was drowning myself in my third beer. The sun had been officially down for about half an hour, but a faint afterglow hung in the sky.

Talia, running late after a deans' meeting that had gone on for an hour past its scheduled cutoff, had stopped at the restaurant on her way home and grabbed a little bit of everything off their menu. What we didn't stuff ourselves with tonight we'd employ as leftovers for the next several days.

"What do you mean, happens now?" I asked.

I was in full lounge mode: sweats, tee-shirt, and athletic socks. My cutie, no doubt famished after her over-long meeting, had merely kicked off her flats had shed her suit jacket, leaving her still about ten times overdressed compared to me.

"I mean," she said, "I'm assuming the TV show is a no-go now?"

"I'm not sure it ever was a go," I said. "You no doubt picked up on it the other night that, while Wendy appeared to have something of a business head on her, Carson was pretty much a . . ."

"Flake?" Talia offered.

"Yeah, that's about it."

"And he's disappeared?"

"Don't know if he did it intentionally," I said, "but in a town this size it's kind of significant the cops didn't find him right away. Best guess is he's not wandering around footloose and fancy free."

"You know for sure the police haven't found him? They have no obligation to keep you up to date, do they?"

"Obligation? No, not really. But I've known Nichols a long time, plus Santiago doesn't seem to hate me quite as much as he used to."

"You did help him out quite a bit a while back," Talia said.

"Yeah, but I eventually got my going fee for the Marlowe deal. Santiago put me down as a consultant, so it's not like he owes me. But even so, he doesn't glower quite as much when I'm around."

"And Carson hasn't reached out to you?" Talia asked.

I shook my head. "No real reason why he should. It's not like we're best buds or anything. We hardly know each other."

"Except he doesn't know anyone else in the area," Talia said.

I shrugged. "Far as I know, but we didn't really get into that. For all I know, he's got a whole posse of old college buddies or something. But with a, as you consider him, flake like that, it's kind of hard to predict anything he will or won't do."

We stopped talking for a few minutes to concentrate on chowing down. I was gratified that Talia had ordered a double helping of orange chicken, mainly because I know she doesn't care for the dish at all, which meant she got it specifically for me. We split an eggroll and had a crab Rangoon each before she came back to the main topic.

"Then you don't see this causing you any trouble?" she asked.

"Don't know why it would. I barely know the people and have nothing to do with whatever their problems were."

Talia pursed her lips.

"What?" I asked.

She took a second before answering, a little notch forming between her eyes. "I spent even less time with them than you, but Mr. Carson didn't exactly strike me as the murderous type."

"I would agree," I said. "Then again, what is the murderous type?"

Talia cocked her head as she considered that. "His being missing does kind of count in favor of his guilt, doesn't it?"

"It does," I said, "but there are other possible explanations."

"Such as?"

I paused to take another drink of my beer. As I did so, Talia speared a pork dumpling and plopped it in her mouth. "The most obvious alternate explanation is he's lying dead somewhere as well."

"You think that?"

"Could be. Or it could be he's off on a lark of some kind and doesn't know anything about it yet."

"Except," Talia said, "according to you the cops have been trying to call his cell phone."

"They've been trying," I said.

"Can't they track it through the towers or something like that? That's what you always hear on the news."

"They could. If he has it with him, and if he didn't break it and toss it in the trash. For whatever reason, they can't get a read on it."

"And as far as you know, he doesn't have any connections out here at all."

"Except that one of their interns is from this area," I said.

"From Providence?"

"Don't know for sure. He just said she was from around here."

"Any other possibilities?" Talia asked.

"He could be hurting somewhere and unable to get help. Could have met a woman to shack up with. Hell, could be drunk at some unknown friend's house, for all I know."

Talia took a couple of bites of Lo Mein while I munched some more orange chicken.

"I guess the good news is," she said, "that it's really none of your business. The cops are on it, and you're not officially involved with either of those people, right?"

"Right," I said, "but a damned shame though."

Talia gave me a quizzical look. "How so?"

"This may have been my one shot at stardom gone down the drain," I said with a touch of sarcasm.

CHAPTER TEN

I WAS PROVEN SOMEWHAT WRONG WHEN JOHN Carson called me the next morning.

I'd spent the night at Talia's, then zoomed over to my place for a shower, breakfast, and change of clothes. I would have had breakfast with her, but she had an early appointment with a major moneybags who was thinking of donating the equivalent of my annual income for a century to the Social Sciences College. We went our separate ways around seven thirty, which had me entering The Blaster right about nine.

Things were up and running, with a larger than normal number of clients for that time of the morning. I waved to Lisa, who was helping a sixtyish woman with one of the machines, and headed back to my office. I'd barely had time to make a cup of coffee, sit down, and contemplate the day ahead when my cell buzzed.

My phone pegged the number as unknown, and at first I intended to ignore it as that type of call is usually someone either trying to take your money or get your opinion on the current state of politics in America. Since I didn't feel like parting with any funds and had some years back about given up on trying to figure out the state of politics in America, I usually don't bother with unknown number calls.

However, on a hunch, I picked this one up.

"Hey, is this you Quinton?" a shaky voice asked.

"Sure is."

"It's me, John Carson."

I took a deep breath.

"Where are you, John? What have you been doing?"

"I've been out and about. You know, seeing the sites."

"We don't have a whole lot of sites to see around here," I said.

"Yeah, well. You've gotta help me, Sam. I didn't shoot Wendy."

I paused for a second.

Interesting choice of words on his part.

"The cops have been looking for you, John."

"I know, and if they find me they're going to be looking at me hard."

"But you're innocent," I said.

"Of course I am, Sam. You know me, buddy. I wouldn't do such a thing."

I considered pointing out to him I barely knew him at all, and for sure wouldn't count him as a buddy, but figured it wasn't the right time. The guy was spooked. I could hear the tremors clearly when he spoke.

"If you've been out and about," I said, "how'd you know she was killed?"

Now it was Carson's turn to hesitate. "I was somewhere where I heard people talking, so I looked it up on the news."

"The local paper's website?" I asked.

"Yeah, the Times or some such name."

I took in another deep breath. Common sense here would be to get an address out of him and notify the cops. But I had the hunch if I disengaged now he'd be gone for good.

"I read their story, John," I said. "It mentioned her death as suspicious. It didn't say anything about her being shot."

"I guess I just assumed. Suspicious death means murder, right? How else would she have been killed?"

I guessed there was some logic there, but at the moment I didn't feel up to exploring it. "If you didn't do it, John, go ahead and turn yourself in. Get it cleared up."

"You're kidding, right? Wendy and I are from out of town, all the hell the way over on the West Coast. Don't know anyone around here at all. You think the cops are going to blink twice before putting me away?"

"They'll follow procedure, sure. But I can put you in touch with a good lawyer who will . . ."

"I don't need a lawyer, big guy. I need you."

"Excuse me?"

"You're a PI, right? A mystery solver? Well, here's a mystery that needs solving. I want someone to prove my innocence. You up for it?"

"John," I said, "this isn't the way to go about things. Go to the cops. They'll question you, look into it, and if you're clean, they'll clear you. They can investigate something like this a whole lot better and quicker than I can."

"Are you kidding, big guy? Don't you know cops are just itching to pin something on an innocent person? You know, in order to protect the crooked interests that pull their strings? How do you not know this stuff?"

"Why would any powerful people in mid Missouri be concerned about a producer from Hollywood?" I asked.

"It's all connected, guy. All part of one large, crooked scheme."

I shook my head. "Tell you what," I said. "This isn't working over the phone. Why don't we get together and talk things over?"

I counted to five before Carson replied. "Okay, big guy. But no cops. I see any cops around and I'm gone."

My first inclination was, as soon as the call ended, to call Josh Nichols, but something tickled at the back of my brain.

"John," I said, "tell me again you didn't kill Wendy."

"I didn't man. Swear to God."

"But?"

I could hear Carson take in a long, deep breath. "But I'm pretty sure I know who did. Which is why I'm insisting on no cops."

I had a feeling in my gut I was really going to regret my next words. "Okay, then. Let's get together."

CHAPTER ELEVEN

"THE MAFIA?" I ASKED, STRUGGLING TO keep a straight face. Carson nodded as he munched on some French fries.

The guy pretty much looked like hell. His black dress shirt was soiled and wrinkled; his suit jacket looked like it had been slept in; and his hair hadn't seen a comb in at least a day.

Plus, he'd shown up with red-rimmed watery eyes.

We'd gotten together at a local Five Guys, ordered lunch, then sat down at a table in the far back, behind the soda machine. At first Carson had fidgeted. Then, after I'd gone up to the counter and gotten our food, he began to open up a bit.

"The Mafia," I repeated. "You think they killed Wendy?"

After nodding emphatically, he now began shaking his head. He took a sip of his soda. "Maybe not the actual organization," he said, "but for sure one of their connections."

"And you think this why?" I asked, a small part of my mind wondering why I was wasting my time.

Carson dipped his head a bit, and I wondered if he was going to go back to eating rather than answer my question. "Wendy and I had our duties divvied up pretty good. Why we were such a good team. I handled the creative side of things while she dealt with the business end."

"I already got that," I said, though in my opinion applying the word "creative" to himself may have stretched things a bit.

He took a bite of his burger and chewed it a little too quickly. I prodded him a little.

"What all is involved with the business side?"

Carson waved his hand in a kind of aimless way. "You know, all the boring stuff. Contracts, purchasing, dividing up the royalty splits, ancillary deals. All that sort of stuff."

To me a better word instead of "boring" would have been "necessary," but again I let it slide.

"How's the business doing?" I asked, mainly to keep him talking.

Carson had made it halfway through his burger, but he put it down, wiped his hands on a couple of napkins and leaned back in his chair. "That's the thing, Sam. That's what I could never quite wrap my head around."

"How so?"

"When I first came to your gym, I rattled off the titles of some of our shows over the last few years."

"Yeah?"

"And you hadn't heard of any of them," Carson said.

"Don't take it personally, John. Truth be told, reality TV's not quite my thing."

Carson shook his head, a kind of desperate look creeping into his eyes. "No, man, you don't get it. Even if you were a dedicated reality freak, you know, all day all the time, like a goddamned shut in, I'd be willing to bet you still wouldn't have heard of any of our shows."

My food was probably getting cold, but I had an idea where he was going and didn't want to break the chain of conversation. "John, have you guys actually had any programs get on the air?"

"On the air?" Carson said. "You mean, as in actually broadcast?"

"Uh huh.

"Sure, one or two, mainly overseas."

"In Europe?"

"Depends on what you mean by Europe." Carson's shoulders had drooped as we talked. "A few years back, we had one that did pretty well in Lithuania for about a season and a half."

"Are you guys in the red?"

"Not exactly in the red, but most years we barely break even."

I'd hardly touched my food, but I pushed my tray off to the side.

"Didn't you kind of wonder about that? About how your firm managed to keep going?"

Carson shook his head, though not with a lot of emphasis. "At first, I guess I assumed Wendy was good with numbers, you know. Figured she had ways of finding us lines of credit to keep going."

I had a flash image of how tickled Lisa Nolan would be if I had such a casual attitude to running The Blaster. Then again, as it was, Lisa did most of the managing herself. If I was of a mind to spend my days prancing around doing whatever, it would be like Heaven for her.

I wondered if Carson had actually thought about it much or if he was so enamored with the idea of being a TV producer that he blindly overlooked hard truths.

"Lately, though," he said, "I've been thinking kind of different."

"How so?" I asked.

Carson stared at his food for a moment. "I don't really know when, but it kind of came to me there was something going on behind the scenes. Something Wendy was keeping from me."

"Like what?"

He shrugged. "Like something crooked going on. Tell you the truth, guy, I was kind of scared to ask her. Figured what I didn't know wouldn't hurt me."

I could see a guy like him thinking that way.

"Kind of changed my mind when I saw her lying there dead though," he said a moment later.

I tensed up. "You saw her?"

He nodded and went back to wolfing down his burger and fries. I waited till he came up for air.

"John," I said, keeping my voice low and hoping he'd take the hint to do the same, "the cops have been looking for you for almost forty-eight hours. You haven't been in your hotel room, and from what you told me you don't know anyone in the area."

"Yeah, well," he said.

I looked him over for a second, wondering again at how used up and thrown out he looked. "Carson," I asked, "have you been driving around for the last day or so?"

Finished with his burger and fries, he pushed his tray to the side of the table next to mine. "I guess I have been. I thought of trying to get another hotel to lie low for a while but decided in a town this size I'd be found pretty damned quick."

Yet somehow, he'd managed to skate around town unnoticed while driving a sky-blue Corvette.

"How and when did you see her body?" I asked.

Carson placed his palms flat on the table, his arms straight out. For a moment, he strained there, then he began to shake—first his forearms, then his upper arms, and finally his entire torso.

I expected to see tears coming at any point, but he managed to keep those at bay.

"She texted me a couple of hours after we got back to the hotel from dinner the other night. Said she wanted to go over some business stuff before we got too far in negotiating with you."

"I thought you said she handled all the business."

He nodded, and though his face tightened up, still no tears.

Maybe John Carson was a tougher man than I'd given him credit for.

"She did. That's why it seemed weird. I even said so. 'Wendy,' I said, 'you handle all the money stuff, not me.' But she said this time was different and she wanted my input."

"So you went to her room?"

Carson nodded hard enough I felt he would snap his neck. "When she didn't answer, I went on in."

"Wait a minute," I said. "How'd you get in? Hotel room doors close and lock automatically."

"Sure, but when you check in, most places give you two keys. Wendy and I always swapped keys with each other."

I peered at him. "Why?"

"Huh?"

"Were you guys involved?" I asked.

"What, me and Wendy? Huh uh."

"Then why did you need each other's room keys?"

Carson sat all the way back and stared at me, giving me a look that held maybe a small smidgen of actual intelligence in it. "I don't know," he said. "Wendy always said it was a good idea. We've done it for years."

I skulled that one over. If both partners were straight business people, it didn't make a lot of sense, especially considering they were opposing genders.

But if one of them had some concern for their safety, it could have been, at least until now, an effective technique.

"Did either of you ever make use of the other's keys?" I asked.

"You mean did we ever enter the other's room when they weren't there?" Carson asked.

"That's right."

A rather guilty look flickered over Carson's face. He glanced down to his tray and twirled it around for a couple of revolutions. It reminded me of when I was a kid and my mom caught doing something I shouldn't have been, how I would look down at the ground and dig my toe into the carpet.

"Carson?" I asked.

He looked back up, slumped his shoulders, and puffed out a gust of air. "Okay, sometimes I'd sneak into her room when she was out and order up some champagne or something, then take it to my room."

I wanted to shake my head hard enough to snap me back into the real world. "Why would you do that?"

Now he gave another look, one I couldn't begin to classify. "It was just something to do for kicks, you know? Get something expensive and have it on her bill, not mine."

I took a moment to work it through. "What difference would it make? The bills were all being paid by the company, right?"

"Well, sure. But this way the really expensive stuff would be comped to Wendy's room."

"I still don't get it. For what reason?"

He sent me a sickly grin, as if struggling to keep things light and not quite succeeding. "It was just a gag, Quinton. You know. See how long it would take before she caught on."

"And how often did you pull this little stunt?" I asked.

He brought his hand up in a flat plane and wagged it back and forth. "Probably about once every time we had an out-of-town trip."

"She ever catch on? Ever say anything to you?" I asked.

Now his expression turned slightly down. "Naw, she never did. Sometimes I would go all out, ordering caviar and crap like that and having it stuck on her bill, but she never noticed."

A possibility floated into my head. It sounded kind of ridiculous, but it was a scenario that could possibly fit the circumstances, including Carson's seemingly ridiculous reference to the Mafia.

"Maybe she did," I said.

"Huh?"

"It may be partial proof of what you're telling me," I said. "If she really was using your company for something underhanded, maybe she saw the expenses you were running up and didn't give a damn."

"Why would that be?" he asked. "If the company lost money, she lost money. What good would it do to ignore expenses that way?"

"Well," I said, "and understand I haven't thought this through and I'm for sure not an expert in this field."

"Okay," Carson said.

"But one thing does come to mind, as a possibility, is money laundering."

Carson stared at me for a moment, his eyes unclouded, and for the first time in our brief association I had the feeling I was dealing with a real, thinking human being.

He took a minute to think it through before giving a half nod.

"She didn't care about expenses," he said, "because it was all going to come out in the wash."

"So to speak," I said.

CHAPTER TWELVE

The idea did seem like a stretch. But while I didn't swallow it completely, I couldn't really dismiss the idea outright.

If Wendy Truell had been using Monumental Productions to do something criminal, such as laundering money, I doubted it would be for the old-time Mafia. From what little I knew of the old syndicates, mainly from direct experience and contact with their counterparts around Missouri, they had traditional, well-established methods of cleaning their cash, and I couldn't see either Wendy Truell or John Carson fitting into their game plan.

Maybe Wendy, if in fact she had been the level-headed businesswoman she appeared on first meeting her, but no traditional gangsters worth anything would have put up with a goofball like Carson being anywhere near their operation.

More than likely, if Carson was on the level, it would be some of the newer, less organized cartels who would make use of Wendy's services. While I didn't know anyone at all in that line of work, I did know someone who could possibly help point me in the right direction.

If I wanted to go in that direction at all. The truth is cops are usually pretty darned good at their jobs, and their instincts most of the time spot-on, and any cop at all would have said right away the odds were heavy the guy sitting across the table from me was Wendy's killer, and as such I really didn't want to have anything more to do with him.

Gangster stories and conspiracies are fine and all that, but most often the simplest and most direct answer is the correct one.

The obvious next step was to call Josh Nichols, turn Carson over, and call it a day. Let Santiago and his guys and gals sort it out.

Hell, that's what they were paid for.

It's the kind of thing I was sometimes paid for as well, but at the moment the only possible client in sight who would want me involved was probably only a step or two away from insolvency.

"Let's call the cops, John, and get you square with them."

He lurched back in his chair, glancing both ways. "No, man, I told you. The cops will nail me for this as sure as . . ."

"Did you kill her?" I asked.

Carson snorted. I don't think I've ever actually heard anyone snort before.

"'Course I didn't, Sam. Haven't you been listening? She was the meal ticket. She's what kept me living the high life. Why would I dust her?"

I've also never heard anyone use the word "dust" in the way he had, and I wondered how long it had been since Carson had visited anything remotely resembling the real world.

"If you didn't," I said, "then there's nothing to worry about. We'll go in, get you squared away, and they can go about finding who really killed Wendy."

"They'll pin me in her hotel room. Through fingerprints or DNA or whatever."

I sighed, even a couple of days with John Carson wearing my patience down to about nothing. "So what? You were her business partner. You guys were traveling together, and you had a key to her room."

"You don't think they'll find it suspicious?" Carson asked.

"Probably. But so what? It's a long leap to murder. Among other things, they'd have to come up with some sort of motive. Especially considering that she was keeping your business going, any reason at all you would have had to be on the outs with her?"

"Naw, man. Not at all. It's not like we were ex-lovers or anything, just business partners. And like you said, without her there wouldn't have been much of a business."

"Then trust me. They'll be glad to be able to cross you off their list."

He looked rather doubtful, and I wondered if he were about to launch into another of his fantasy tirades. For some reason, maybe because he was becoming fatigued after the last twenty-four hours he'd had, he nodded.

Maybe Carson, for once, was dealing with reality.

"Okay," he said, "give 'em a call. But if they railroad me into prison in an effort to make themselves look good in the press, I'll remind you this was your idea."

Then again, maybe not.

"Let me make some calls," I said.

CHAPTER THIRTEEN

A LITTLE AFTER TWO THAT AFTERNOON, CARSON and I walked into the detectives squad room of the main Riverside police station, downtown a few blocks from Main Street. The moment we stepped into the room Josh Nichols, from his desk situated next to Lt. Santiago's enclosed office, noticed us and stood up.

A couple of other detectives glanced our way, but with Nichols being the second in command of the squad they didn't pay us much attention.

Nichols was wearing dark brown slacks with a light tan shirt and no tie. His sleeves were rolled up to his elbows, and I noticed a couple of smudges under his eyes.

"Rough night?" I asked while Carson, according to my instructions before we entered the building, didn't say anything.

I should try that more often, as Carson not talking made my whole day brighter.

"Rough night and morning," Nichols said. "It's not every day we get an entertainment big shot murdered in town, and City Hall is noticeably interested."

I glanced over at Santiago's office. The three walls were of glass from about waist-level up. The office was empty with the lights off.

"That explain where the boss man is?" I asked.

"Yup." Nichols nodded. "He's meeting with the powers that be right now, trying to convince them we're not a bunch of rubes around here." For the first time since we walked up to his desk,

Nichols turned his eye directly on Carson. "I thought you didn't have a clue where he was."

"I didn't, Josh. Not till he called me a couple of hours ago."

"Which you, being the upright citizen we all know you are, made us aware of right away."

"What's it matter an hour, give or take? Here's your guy, and I even saved the department the time and gas money of bringing him in."

Nichols looked at us for a minute, then jerked his head towards Santiago's office, and Carson and I followed him in there.

Once inside, Nichols shut the door, though I noticed he didn't lower any of the blinds, and leaned himself against the desk with his arms folded across his chest. "Let's have it," he said.

"Carson says he didn't do it, Josh."

"Well, hell buddy. Why'd you bother bringing him in then? A phone call would have done just as well."

"Josh," I began.

"Can it, Blondie. I want to hear it from the man himself." He now bent his gaze directly at Carson. "Did you kill her?"

"No."

"What about . . ."

"Sorry, Josh," I interrupted. "That's all he's going to say until Bernie Lyman shows up."

"Blondie . . ."

"Look," I said. "You wanted the guy to present himself, and here he is. He came in voluntarily. He told me his story. He's not going to clam up; he's not going to be hostile to you guys. But you and I both know no one, especially in a case this serious, should talk to the cops without a lawyer around. That's all we're waiting on."

If I wasn't such a tough guy, Nichols's glower would have cut me in two. As it was, I held my ground. "If it helps at all, I called Lyman right after I called you. He should be here any moment."

"At which point your boy here," he jerked his thumb in Carson's direction, "is going to come clean with us."

"At which point he's going to follow his lawyer's advice," I said.

"Lieutenant's going to love this."

"He should," I said, "because we're safeguarding that your case somewhere down the line won't fall apart because of any overzealousness on the part of the police."

"Seriously, Blondie? Overzealous. You using two-syllable words now?"

Before I could answer, Carson spoke up. "I don't get it, Sam. I thought you said the sergeant here was a friend of yours."

"He is," I said. "He's being a little grumpy at the moment."

"A little grumpy?" Nichols's voice went up a notch. "You want to see grumpy, why don't we . . ."

Before he could finish his thought there was a knock on the door. As intent as we'd been on arguing we hadn't noticed anything going on outside the office's glass walls.

Coming right after the knock, the office door opened and Bernie Lyman, one of the hottest criminal attorneys in the state, stuck his head in.

"Mind if I join you fellows?" he asked.

CHAPTER FOURTEEN

BERNIE LYMAN HAD SHOWN UP ABOUT ten minutes after Carson and I arrived at the station. This wasn't an indication of his desire for work, especially as Bernie's pretty much considered the premier defense attorney in the central part of the state. More, it was an indication of how small a city Providence is, and the fact that in the right conditions any two points in town are no more than fifteen minutes apart.

Actually, I was kind of surprised it took Bernie as long to get there as it did. Especially considering his office is only about six blocks away from the station. But I figured he'd been having an extremely late lunch and let it go.

Edging into his late fifties, Bernie's been at the lawyer game for quite a while. He doesn't look much like the firecracker he is. Short, not even five eight, and kind of skinny. With his wrinkled and ragged clothing, he comes across most of the time as about two steps away from homelessness.

"How's it going, Sam?" he asked, his beaming, used car salesman smile making clear he was one of the last handful of smokers on earth. His gaze turned to fix on Carson. "I'm guessing this is my new client."

"Bernie Lyman, John Carson," I said. Neither man made a move to shake hands, instead giving each other slight nods.

"Carson's a television producer," I said.

Bernie took a double look. "Named John Carson?"

"That's his name," I said.

"Why's that surprising to everyone?" Carson asked.

Bernie shook his head and turned to Nichols. "Do we have any paperwork on our friend here?"

"Not yet. You got here before we got very far."

"Charges?" Bernie asked.

As the two of them started talking back and forth, with Carson standing off to the side looking confused, I figured my work was done. I said my goodbyes to everyone, assured Carson he was in the best of hands, and left the squad room.

I had total faith in Lyman's ability to look after the problem, and since the cops were going all out on Wendy Truell's murder, time to get back to running my gym.

Or at least, get back to running as much of it as Lisa would let me do. Lisa's been with me quite a while, making the transition all the way from client with a messy personal life to hourly worker who got her act together to manager. There was a time when I used to run the whole place myself, but any more I couldn't imagine doing it without her around.

She's a short five two, but height doesn't signify anything about her capability. Her red hair and green eyes, however, do truthfully indicate something about her temper if she gets to going.

Today, she was wearing long black shorts and a loose green tee-shirt. She has the figure to pull off the highest end of workout clothes but has this thing about not wanting to overshadow the female clients.

"This mean there's not going to be a TV show?" she asked once I'd filled her in on the highlights of my last twenty-four hours.

"That's the main concern?" I asked. "Whether there's going to be a show or not?"

She shrugged and did her best to not look too disappointed. "Would have been great publicity for this place."

I took a deep breath. "Lisa, he wanted to relocate the business to the Lake and have me working out of a seedy storefront."

"Huh?"

"That was kind of my reaction," I said.

"Okay, there would have been a few wrinkles to work out. No biggee."

I shook my head and headed back to my office.

Maybe a couple of hours of checking over invoices would help clear my head from John Carson and company.

Turned out such was not to be, though, because I'd barely had time to pour myself a cup of coffee and turn on my computer when someone knocked on the door.

"Come in," I said, assuming it was Lisa with some minor errand, even though she usually barged right in as if she owned the place, which one of these days she probably will.

The door opened, and suddenly my fairly easy afternoon got a whole lot more complicated.

Sean O'Flaherty walked into my office.

"Quinton," he said.

"Sean," I replied, wondering what the hell he wanted.

Nothing to brighten your day like a visit from the area's number one mobster.

CHAPTER FIFTEEN

"**B**EEN A WHILE," I SAID.

O'Flaherty nodded and took a seat in one of the two chairs arranged in front of my desk. He looked around for a moment.

The Irishman's a bit older than me, somewhere in his early to mid-fifties. I'm not sure his exact age, and I doubt anyone who knows his rep is foolish enough to ask him. Despite being in the latter stage of middle age, at just under six feet he stays in shape and carries his weight well.

Even if he was a complete roly poly, though, you probably couldn't tell it because he wears clothes tailored from the most exclusive shop in Providence. The kind of place that sells shirts, when they're on sale, for a couple of hundred dollars apiece.

His outfit today was a midnight-blue two-piece suit, judging by its sheen made from silk; a dark gray shirt, also no doubt silk; and black mesh loafers.

Come to think of it, the only person I know who dresses anywhere near as well is Lieutenant Santiago.

O'Flaherty has sharp blue eyes and sandy blond hair that's thinning a bit, though far as I could tell it hadn't receded any more than the last time I saw him.

"Place looks about the same," he said.

"Well, it hasn't been that long."

The mobster grinned. Even though I knew him for a cold-hearted gangster, I never could work up much dislike for the man.

"What you been up to?" he asked.

"Little of this, little of that. What can I do for you, Sean?"

He narrowed his eyes a little at my use of his first name but must have decided to let it go. "I've been asked to look into something by some —friends of mine."

"Okay."

"And it turns out that something involves you."

I pretty much had guessed right off why he showed up but decided to make him work for it a little. "Involves me? How is that?"

O'Flaherty grinned. He was the kind of guy who could give you either a warm, friendly grin or one that would practically peel the skin right off your bones. Fortunately, this was his warm grin.

Well, maybe lukewarm.

"We're not going to play games, are we Sam?" he asked.

I shook my head, leaned back in my chair, and crossed my hands behind to rest my head in them. "Should I guess we're talking about John Carson?"

"A friend of a friend reached out to me this morning," he said.

"Didn't know you had any business on the West Coast."

"I don't," O'Flaherty said. "But the Kansas City boys do."

"Not to mention the Los Angeles boys."

"Not to mention."

"And could I guess," I said, "that it's not really Carson these friends of friends are worried about but Wendy Truell."

O'Flaherty's expression was that of a man who didn't have a care in the world. "If that's the name of the guy's business partner, sure. Shows how far out of the loop I am."

I nodded, and the two of us spent a few seconds looking at each other.

"So what's the story, Sam?" he finally asked.

"I don't know even close to half of it, but I'll tell you what I do know." I gave him a brief rundown of my association with Carson and Truell, ending with leaving the police station a few minutes before he showed up.

"And that's all of it?" O'Flaherty asked.

"All of my end, at least."

O'Flaherty frowned. "Something's left out," he said.

A faint pricking started along the back of my neck. "Not by me, Sean."

"If not by you, then by the cops. Or maybe this Carson person."

Now it was my turn to frown. "I don't follow. What are you talking about?"

"Again," he said, "I'm not personally involved with any of this."

"Right. Just helping out a friend of a friend."

O'Flaherty nodded. "But even from what little information I'm working with, something isn't computing in your story."

"Like what?" I asked.

"Like the three million."

The prickling now became a full-on assault by army ants. "What three million?"

O'Flaherty took a deep breath and sat up straighter in his chair. "A couple of hours after the Truell woman left the coast, some folks determined certain funds recently provided to her were missing."

"Certain funds," I said.

"Yes."

"There's a little suspicion she was doing some work for some criminal elements out there," I said.

"If by doing work, you're talking about cleaning up their money, I'd say that's a pretty good guess. Off the record, of course."

"Of course. You're saying she took some money to wash, and made off with it? Came out here?"

O'Flaherty grinned and removed an invisible speck of lint from his pants leg. "I'm not attesting to anything like that, Quinton. After all, that would be admitting to knowledge of some sort of criminal conspiracy. I'm merely passing along gossip."

"Three million bucks would be a heck of a motive for murder," I said.

"Yes, it would."

"But there's a couple holes in your gossip," I said.

O'Flaherty grinned even wider. I felt like a schoolboy being pushed by the teacher to think for myself. "Such as?"

"For one, three million dollars is an awful lot of money."

"For some people," O'Flaherty said.

"For most people. And while I've never attempted it myself, I'd guess carting around that much in cash would take a couple of suitcases."

"Depends on the size of the bills," O'Flaherty pointed out.

"True, but with the way banks and such are cracking down these days, it's getting to where passing anything more than a twenty is a tough proposition. If she had three mill in small bills, it would fill multiple suitcases. And if she had bigger bills, it would be almost impossible to use them."

"There are other ways to carry funds around," O'Flaherty said.

"You mean something like a cashier's check?"

"Would be a lot more convenient."

"It would," I said, "but you'd have to have a whole lot of them. Again, it's not like the old days. Get them for too large a value and there's going to be questions raised."

"Okay," O'Flaherty said, "what about bearer bonds?"

"Come on, Sean. You know more about this stuff than I do, and even I know bearer bonds went out decades ago, about the time the IRS came into the twentieth century."

O'Flaherty grinned. "Not bad, Quinton. Regardless of you shooting down all my ideas, the fact remains that according to rumor, she somehow made off with all that money from people who want it back. That's the way it is."

"Maybe," I said, "if not for the other hole in the idea."

"Which is?"

"If someone, hypothetically, was planning on robbing some faction of organized crime to the tunes of millions of dollars, what would be the point of obviously and clearly traveling out here to Providence? For what?"

O'Flaherty grinned, and I was a little relieved to see it was a grin of pure amusement, not some malicious expression.

"We still speaking hypothetically?" he asked.

"Far as I'm concerned. Hell, I don't even have a real client in all this. I'm about as uninvolved as you can get."

"Word I had was the Truell woman's partner was your client," O'Flaherty asked.

"He kind of wanted to be, but I didn't see any reason for it. I got hold of a good lawyer to defend him with the cops and went my way."

"Who'd you get?"

I thought about it for a minute but didn't see any reason not to tell. After all, if it already wasn't it would soon be public record soon. "I called Bernie Lyman to come down and help him out."

O'Flaherty nodded. "Makes sense. Lyman's good. We've tried to hire him more than once ourselves. Okay, then. Again, hypothetically, I would guess any 'interested parties' would be confused as all hell about why the woman would steal from them only to come out to a middle America place like this."

"And would it be a stretch," I asked, "to assume they would ask someone they were familiar with to look into it?"

O'Flaherty nodded again. "Could be. But if you had taken a bundle like that, from people with short tempers, where would you head off to?"

"Somewhere as far away as I could get. But we're talking in circles here. If she took the three mill, in whatever form, where the hell is it and why come here?"

"That's what a few of my business associates would like to know."

I spread my hands out. While I took it as a good sign that Sean hadn't come with any of his goons, still no reason to cause unnecessary trouble. "What's that got to do with me, Sean? You don't think I have the money, do you?"

O'Flaherty chuckled. I've heard more comforting sounds in my time.

"No, Sam, of course not. I wanted to let you know I've been tasked with helping to clear all this up."

"One more question," I said.

"Yeah?"

"Wouldn't it have been smarter of them to get their money back before killing her?"

O'Flaherty frowned. "Yeah, that's kind of got us confused. The bosses don't mind brokering some deals here and there, but it kind of looks like someone back west is playing games."

"And of course, they're all such upstanding, honest citizens," I said.

The mobster grinned. "True, though you can't entirely trust them too far."

I thought the situation over for a moment. "Seems to me, the key to the whole thing is why she came out here right after taking that money. If she did."

"I agree," O'Flaherty said, giving me a serious look. "And it would probably help everyone involved if someone could get to the bottom of things."

Gee, I wonder who he meant.

CHAPTER SIXTEEN

I MADE A QUICK CALL TO BERNIE Lyman. While he was serving as John Carson's attorney, he couldn't tell me a whole lot about how things were going, but he did relay to me that he and Carson had just walked out of the station.

"They let him go? He's not a suspect?" I'd asked Bernie.

"Of course he's a suspect," Bernie had said. "But they didn't have much choice but to let him walk."

"How come?"

"So far," Bernie said, "they've turned up nothing in the way of physical evidence, though it's early yet, and while he doesn't have an alibi worth shit, the lack of an alibi isn't evidence of anything."

"Except that the guy's a flake," I pointed out.

Over the phone, I could almost hear Bernie's smirk. "Yeah, he is kind of loosely wrapped, isn't he?"

"If he's even wrapped at all."

"Maybe," Bernie said, "but when you get right down to it, there isn't yet any evidence linking John to the killing."

"Other than common sense," I said. "Assuming Wendy doesn't have any family or acquaintances in the area."

"Far as I can tell on that, the answer's no. Turns out she's originally from Provo, Utah, and has never even visited our fair state in the past."

"Then the only person in the area who knows her, aside from me and Talia, is Carson."

"True," Bernie said. "Regardless, the best they could do for the moment is give him the standard 'don't leave town' oration and let him walk. Though they did it with squinty eyes. You ever had Nichols squint his eyes at you?"

"A time or two, yeah," I said.

"So you know what that can be like. I had to fight myself not to laugh, but it looked like it threw an extra little scare into Carson. By the way, you know his name's not John Carson don't you?"

"Huh?"

"Yep. The last few days you've been wined and dined by Samuel Lemwitz, known as Sammie around his old neighborhood."

"And where's the old neighborhood?" I asked.

"Pasadena far as I can tell."

"With a name like Lemwitz, he probably really stuck out in Pasadena."

"Maybe," Bernie said, "though he strikes me as the kind of guy to make sure he sticks out wherever he is."

"Waitaminit, Bernie. Is he using Carson as a stage name, or whatever the equivalent would be?"

"Nope. He had it legally changed about ten years ago."

"You mean a guy who works in television actually changed his name to John Carson?"

This time, I didn't have to visualize Bernie's smirk. He flat out tittered over the phone. "I made some reference about the irony of that, and it went right over his head. Like I said, the wrapping's kind of loose on this guy."

"But at least he's out for now?" I asked.

"Yep. Though safe to say they're going to be keeping a close eye on him."

"They come up with a possible motive yet?" The thought of O'Flaherty's supposed three million dollars danced through my head.

"Not that they relayed to me, which means either no or they're not sure. I have to tell you, though, Sam, I'm not entirely sure my new client is all there in the head. If he did kill her, who knows why? Maybe one of their shows lost a ratings point and he went off."

"Doubtful," I said, "the way I get it, none of their programs, those that make it to air, do well enough to score even a single ratings point. Far as that goes, I may have another theory of the case for you."

"Oh?" The slight lilt in the one word told me I'd caught Bernie's attention.

"Yeah. When you guys were talking, did you have time at all to go into their business arrangement? Their division of duties?"

"Not much, mainly the general relationship between them. Why?"

"Let me tell you about a meeting I just had."

I went through my entire conversation with O'Flaherty. When I was finished, Bernie took a couple of minutes to digest it all.

"A conduit for the mob?" he finally asked.

"Several mobs, to hear Sean tell it. But not the big, established boys. Sounded like he was talking more about the up-and-comers. This help your case any?"

"Too soon to tell," Bernie said. "I've got to think it through. It could at least raise doubts with a jury if we ever had to get that far."

"Unfortunately," I said. "If Sean's info is correct, the three million could also be a hell of a motive."

"And the whole thing could do more harm than good," Bernie pointed out. "We'd have to convince a prelim judge, let alone a jury, John had no inkling of the financial workings of his own business."

"Flip it around, Bernie. You've spent some time with the guy. Would you trust him with what your granddaughter has in her piggy bank?"

"Nope, but mainly because the kid takes from her old man when it comes to frugality. That seven-year-old probably has more in her piggy bank than you do in your checking account, Sam."

"That wouldn't be that much of a feat. Where does it go with John as far as his legal defense is concerned?"

"At the moment, hang tight and see what develops."

"You're not the only one," I said before I rang off.

I sat at my desk and drummed my fingers for another fifteen minutes before deciding to head downtown and lay it all on Nichols's desk.

Somehow, a phone call didn't seem the appropriate way to go. Turns out my cop buddy's reaction was just about what I'd expected.

CHAPTER SEVENTEEN

"**S**EAN FREAKIN' O'FLAHERTY?" NICHOLS ASKED ME. "He's mixed in this somehow?"

I sat still and waited for him to get it out of his system. On my drive over, I'd debated with myself over how much to tell him.

Nichols was wearing tan slacks with a white shirt, sleeves rolled up to the wrists, and a plain tan tie. The tie had been tightly knotted when I'd been there earlier in the day, but at some point he'd loosened it up.

As I'd walked in, I'd noticed Santiago's office was still empty, and the usual vibe around the squad room was diminished a bit.

"O'Flaherty," Nichols repeated. "Christ, I didn't know you two had turned into such good buddies."

"Buddies is kind of strong," I said. "Probably more like distant acquaintances."

"You did a good turn for him back during that Thayer mess," Nichols said.

I glanced over at Santiago's office. It was darkened again, the head man nowhere to be found. "Sure your boss isn't on vacation?" I asked.

Nichols leaned back in his chair. "Forget worrying about our command structure, Blondie. How deep you think O'Flaherty's involved in this current mess?"

"If I had to guess," I said, "seems like he's just doing a favor for a friend."

"Or maybe a friend of a friend?"

"Maybe," I said. "Basically, he wanted to know what I knew about Wendy Truell's death."

"Which would lend some credence to your wild idea she was funneling mob money through their company."

"He went through all that with you?" I asked. Bernie hadn't mentioned Carson had divulged that much to the cops.

Nichols nodded. "After about fifteen minutes of him and Bernie shouting at each other in private. You believe it?"

"Why wouldn't I? Hell, far as that goes it was practically my idea."

Nichols pushed a few papers from one side of his desk to the other. Looking closer, I noticed a little tick developing in his left eye. "Let's put it this way. Your boy there isn't exactly one hundred percent rooted in the real world."

I grinned. "Did you happen to hear any of his ideas for my TV show?"

"You mean like relocating you down to the Lake and having you drive around in a Ferrari? Yeah, I heard some of that."

"Doesn't mean the money laundering thing isn't a real possibility," I said. "

Nichols shook his head. "No, it doesn't. And the fact that in no time at all Sean O'Flaherty shows up at your place kinda reinforces it."

"So what's your next move?" I asked.

"Make some phone calls I've been putting off, then have my people go over that hotel room again. We did our best to track down any of the Truell woman's movements in town, but she doesn't seem to have gone anywhere much."

"When you think about it, she wasn't here all that long. Did you get anything off her phone?"

"Couldn't find one," Nichols said.

I shot him a look. "Come again?"

"No phone anywhere at the scene. Not even an old flip phone, which I hear some people are going back to using."

"Considering she was an executive far from home," I said, "and she was supposedly here on business, the notion she didn't have a phone on her is kind of interesting."

"It is."

"You couldn't find one anywhere?"

"Nope. My guess is whoever killed her took it and dropped it down the nearest sewer."

"Too bad. There could have been info on it to confirm Carson's allegations."

Nichols cocked an eye at me. "Or there could have been something to point to his guilt. We may have let him walk with Lyman yesterday, but he's still the most obvious suspect."

"While you're searching, keep your eye out for three million dollars."

"Come again?"

"Three million bills. Or maybe not bills. May be line of credit, stock certificates, hell even the numbers of a Swiss bank account or two."

Nichols cocked his head and peered at me. "The Truell woman had three million on her when she came to town?"

"Maybe," I said. "In some form or other."

"And where did you come up with this maybe notion of yours?"

"How about we consider it an anonymous tip," I said.

"Christ," Nichols almost spit. "O'Flaherty told you."

"He may have mentioned something about a large denomination."

"You know what you're doing to me Sam? To this unit? If she was walking around with that much cash, or whatever, you've just upped the possible suspects to near infinity."

"Not quite," I said.

"Really? You mind telling me why?"

"Exactly. The question is why."

Nichols slumped back in his chair. He reached up to loosen the knot of his tie even more. "Straighten it up, buddy. You're talking gibberish to me."

I then went through the basics O'Flaherty and I had discussed. The missing money and the question of why, if Wendy had taken it, she'd gone no farther than the central part of the country.

"Maybe she got waylaid before she could go as far as she'd planned," Nichols said.

"Maybe, but something still doesn't feel right."

"Far as that goes, who knows how long they'd had this trip planned to come see you. Maybe she was keeping to some sort of established schedule."

"That's the point, Josh. This wasn't part of her routine. This kind of thing was always done by Carson, not her."

"Could be she took it as a chance to make her break."

"Then why not make it?" I said. "If you've got access to that kind of cash, why go through the song and dance of a business trip? Why not just make a run for it?"

"We could ask your buddy. He seems like he's on top of things."

"I assume you're keeping an eye on him?"

"I don't think you should be privy to all we're doing Sam," Nichols said. "After all, you are working for the guy, right?"

"Working for Carson? Not hardly."

"Really?" The doubt on Nichols's face arched another couple of degrees. "Then why are you here?"

I stood up. "Just wanted to pass on the word about Sean's involvement and give you something to think about. I'll let you guys do all the heavy lifting. A couple of days dealing with a John Carson was more than enough."

"Damn," Nichols said. "Does this mean no TV show?"

"Honestly, Josh. Do you see a guy like me being able to fit into a sports car?"

As I turned to leave, I took another look at Lt. Santiago's empty office.

Something didn't feel quite right there either.

CHAPTER EIGHTEEN

I NOTICED THE TAIL ALMOST AS SOON as I left the station. Providence's downtown is only a couple of blocks wide and a handful of blocks long, meaning it doesn't take too long, even in the middle of a weekday, to get out of it and onto one of our semi-main drags.

I'd barely pulled out of the city parking garage next to the station when I noticed a bright red Mustang, looking only a year or two old, dart out from the curb and swing in behind me. We stopped at a red light on Main Street. When the light turned green, I changed my original intention and turned east instead of west.

The Mustang, which had been right behind me, kept going straight, heading south and toward the university.

I've been at the detecting gig long enough I didn't start breathing easy yet. Sure enough, five blocks farther on, the tail popped up behind me again.

By this point, I was coming up on one of the city's three colleges, a private women's university that's been around for nearly a century. Right to the east of downtown proper, an overhead walkway connects the college from both sides of the street.

I passed under the arch and kept going. There are a whole lot of little side streets in the area I could have ducked into, but if whoever was in the Mustang meant me some kind of harm, I wanted to be as far out of traffic as possible.

I kept heading straight east. In another few minutes, I'd be on the outskirts of town and heading into the country. That was the good news.

The bad news was that once I made it out of town the road I was on formed a fairly straight, if bendy, stretch of highway, with the only turns leading into new housing complexes that lately have sprung up all over the place.

How the hell anyone could afford a brand-new house with current prices was beyond me, but that wasn't here nor there as far as my current problem. All of those complexes eventually wind into dead ends, not what I wanted.

By now, the Mustang wasn't even bothering to mask its presence. An idea occurred to me, and I grabbed my phone and hit a particular number, one I'd never called and had hoped never to.

"Hello," Sean O'Flaherty answered after the second ring.

"It's Quinton," I said. "By any chance, did you send a couple of bully boys to watch my backside?"

O'Flaherty didn't answer for so long I thought we may have been cut off before he finally spoke up. "No, I didn't. Did I have a reason to?"

"Not as far as I know. But someone's been shadowing me for the last fifteen minutes or so. Sure it's not your people?"

As we spoke, I kept one eye on the rearview mirror. As I waited for O'Flaherty's response, I noticed the trailing car speeding up a bit.

I pressed my accelerator down a little. I'd deliberately been going about five miles under the speed limit. If the car behind me contained innocent people, they would take the first opportunity to zip around.

So far, they hadn't zipped. I figured I'd better assume the worst.

"Not my people, Sam," O'Flaherty said. "What are they driving?"

I told him, which got me a snort from the mobster. "You're kidding, right? Who would run a tail in such a conspicuous car?"

"Damned if I know," I said.

"You want me to make a couple of phone calls and see what's up?"

The red car didn't increase its speed to match mine, but it also didn't veer off anywhere. About twenty miles due east was the small town of Churchill. Before that, basically a whole lot of country road that even, in the latter part of the day, didn't have much in the way of consistent traffic.

"If you do make your calls," I said, "do it very carefully."

"Of course," O'Flaherty said. "You think this has to do with your buddy Carson?"

"He's not my buddy. But considering I'm not working on anything else at the moment, my guess would be yes."

"Fair enough. Give me a couple of hours to make those calls."

"A couple of hours?"

"Sometimes these people are hard to track down," O'Flaherty pointed out.

"Gotcha."

"In the meantime, you want me to send anyone out to help you?"

"No thanks. Doesn't hurt to keep in practice."

"Okay. If I hear anything, I'll let you know. If you don't hear from me, no go."

I hung up and tossed the phone into the passenger seat, then reached into the Cherokee's console.

I grabbed my gun and held it down by my right thigh.

About a hundred yards ahead, around another bend in the road and right before coming upon a small village, sat a convenience store with a car wash off to the side. Most of the times I've been down that way, whether day or night, the car wash sat empty.

Okay, then. Time to find some stuff out.

I gunned the Cherokee, whipped it around a couple more bends, screeched into the convenience store parking lot, then angled across and headed to the car wash.

I whipped into the farthest bay from the highway, shut off the ignition, climbed out and angled myself out of the bay and behind the far wall.

Gun in hand, I waited for the red Mustang to find its way to me.

CHAPTER NINETEEN

THE MUSTANG CAME INTO SIGHT a couple of seconds after I'd gotten situated. It slowed down as it came around the last curve and went on past both the convenience store and gas station. I waited, assuming the driver and anyone else with them was focused on the road ahead. A couple of seconds later came a brief squeal of tires and the sudden gunning of an engine. I had no way to know for sure, and it didn't really matter, but I guessed someone in the car had seen a portion of my Cherokee, nestled in the wash bay, out of the corner of their eye.

I set myself, crouching a bit, and gripped my weapon a little firmer, squeezing myself as much as possible against the brick corner of the car wash. I had time to take two long, deep breaths before the Mustang came rocketing into the car wash's parking lot and jerked to a stop right behind my Cherokee.

Both doors whipped open, and two blond men got out of the vehicle. They were almost clones of each other and, especially to my Midwestern eyes, reeked of Southern California: straggly hair every which way, soft tans, mismatched slacks and blazers.

They also looked like serious trouble, mainly because they were both holding 9mm automatics.

They focused on my Cherokee for a moment, then one walked up to the car while another whipped his head around. Since I'm over six feet and way over two hundred pounds, trying to keep myself hidden at the corner while still able to see what they were doing wasn't going to work for very long.

When I'd whipped into the car wash, I'd noticed six or seven cars parked at the convenience store, two at the pumps and the rest up against the building. That meant quite a few bystanders who somehow had to stay out of the line of fire. The only way I could think of for sure to keep all those people safe was to get things over with as quickly as possible.

I turned away from the corner and skittered along the far outer wall of the wash, pressed tightly enough against it I could feel a little bit of scraping on my back from the red bricks. "Look close, he's somewhere around here," I heard one of the men, I assumed the one who'd walked up to my Cherokee, say.

Another half second and I was at the front corner, back still pressed against the wall and taking deep breaths. I didn't really want to shoot anyone, but with one of me and two of them keeping both in sight would get a little tricky.

At the same time, a tiny corner of my mind was wondering who the hell these guys were and why they were after me. Couldn't worry about that at the moment, though, and before either of them could move from their positions, I swung out from behind the end of the building, squatted down, and covered them. "Hold it!" I said, thinking it was too bad John Carson wasn't there with a camera crew.

He would have loved this.

Both of the blond guys whirled at me, leveling their nines as they did so. I didn't really want to take anyone out, but one thing Duke Prowder, my mentor in the detective biz, had drummed into my head was that, if confronted, you never do warning shots.

A squeeze of my finger, and I drilled the closer guy, the one away from my Cherokee, straight in the central mass. He went skittering backwards before doing a half spin and falling on his right side. I turned instantly to the other but managed to hold back my trigger finger.

Number two had taken a step back, his eyes glued to the sight of his partner on the ground. I kept my weapon leveled, waiting to see if he'd give the whole thing up or try to save it. After what felt like forever but was actually only a heartbeat and a half, he looked at me over his shoulder, then dropped his automatic on the ground.

"You next," I said. "Flat in the dirt and stay there." The guy did so. Carson would kill himself for not being here to film this. Out of the corner of my eye, I saw half a dozen people had edged out of the store and were looking our way.

That's what you get in rural areas. In the city, people scurry for cover at the sound of a gunshot, if they even recognize what it is. In the country, they come out to see what all the fuss is about. What they saw, of course, was one big burly guy standing over another flat on the ground while a third guy off to the side was bubbling up blood from a chest wound.

One of the bystanders, an older man wearing faded blue jeans and a checked shirt, decided to get involved. "You need any help, mister?" he yelled out to me. I nodded.

"Call the sheriff, would you. These two tried to kill me." I hoped to both arouse their curiosity even more and, hopefully, make it clear who was the good guy. I didn't want any heroes drawing a bead on me with their deer rifles. The guy who'd called out gave me a wave and pulled his phone out of his pocket.

I had my own phone, of course, but because I didn't want to divert my eye from my prisoner for even a moment, I was more than happy to wait for the sheriff's people to come. Plus, I needed time to figure out what to tell them.

CHAPTER TWENTY

"**W**HY'D YOU SHOOT THE GUY?" DEPUTY Charles Dawg asked me for the third time.

Dawg was a tall, skinny blond guy in his early twenties. He'd been the first on scene, arriving about five minutes after the man in the store had made the call.

The first two times I'd answered him straight up. By the third go-round, I contemplated making some remark about Deputy Dog, but the kid was young enough he probably wouldn't get the joke.

So far, things could have been worse. Upon arriving, the deputies had handcuffed my second attacker and put him in the back of their car. They'd also made a quick inspection of the first guy, concurred with each other he was dead, and made a call for an ambulance.

I was still handcuff-free, which I hoped was a good sign.

In the spirit of cooperation, I decided to give the deputy the same answer I had the first two times. "They were coming after me. With their guns drawn. I did the only thing I could do to save my life."

The deputy frowned as he jotted something down in a small black notepad.

"If you ask the witnesses over there," I pointed towards the convenience store where two of his men had corralled the bystanders, "they'll tell you the same thing."

"According to them, they didn't see much of anything," the deputy said.

"Of course not because they were inside. But they heard and came rushing out in no time."

Dawg frowned even harder and made a couple more notes in his pad even though I hadn't said anything I hadn't already mentioned.

"Did you call Sgt. Nichols?" I asked. While we were technically in the county, I figured bringing in the city was a natural course of action.

"Called him," Dawg said, "haven't heard back yet."

"Nichols is a good guy."

Dawg peered at me a little closer. "I know Nichols. Know about you, far as that goes."

"Oh yeah. Did you recognize me by my bulging biceps?"

Dawg shook his head and ran his hand over his almost-buzz cut head. "Nope. Recognized you first by that mop on top of your head. Aren't you a little old to be wearing your hair that long?"

"What makes you say that?" I asked.

"Well, for one thing, seeing as there's more gray than blond maybe they should start calling you the Silver Stud, or some such."

By this point, Dawg had reclined against his vehicle while three or four of his other men wandered around looking for something to do. He crossed his arms and stared at me. "You got anything more to say about this here situation?"

Before I could answer, a brown Nissan coasted around the closest bend. Right behind it came a Providence PD cruiser, and behind the patrol car an ambulance pulled in.

Three EMT's, two male and one female, got out of the ambulance and, after a quick visual scan of the scene, didn't say a word to the deputies but went right over to the guy I'd shot. The three of them palavered for a minute before one, from my vantage point he looked like the youngest, trotted back to the ambulance. He disappeared inside for a second, then popped out with a body bag and went back to join his comrades.

Quite a party for the locals in the store.

Dawg spoke to one of the other deputies. "Go over there, Pete.

Tell them we can't move the corpse yet until the tech guys and the ME get here."

Pete, a big, goofy-looking blond kid in his early twenties, nodded and headed over to the little knot of activity.

Dawg looked at me. "County EMT's don't get quite as much practice at murder scenes as the city ones."

Nichols climbed out of the Nissan and headed over our way, a sour look on his face.

Dawg turned and held out his hand to Nichols. "How you doin', Josh?"

Nichols returned the shake. "I was better about twenty minutes ago." He jerked a thumb at me. "I'm guessing he's responsible for this?"

"Says they took a run at him and he, ah, fought back."

"He does tend to fight back now and then." Nichols squinted at me. "Anything to add to that, Sam?"

"Only that the deputy here has my weapon, along with the guns he took off the dead guy and his partner."

"Where's the partner?" Nichols asked.

"Got him in the back of our car, one of the other guys watching him."

"Anything else?" Nichols said.

"Not much at the moment," Dawg said. "Except neither of these two guys look exactly local."

Nichols gave me another squint. "This have anything to do with the Truell thing?"

"Don't know why it would," I said. "On the other hand, I'm not working on anything else and, like the deputy here said, they don't look like they're from around here."

Nichols turned back to the deputy. "Had a chance to question the survivor, Chuck?"

"About long enough for him to say the word lawyer. You know how it goes, Josh. After that, we've got to button it up."

"ID on either of them?" Nichols asked.

"Wallets on both, but no identification of any kind. Surivor's not even giving out his name."

Nichols glanced over at the deputy car with the prisoner in the back, then back to me. "Looks almost like a California beach boy," he said.

I nodded. "I had something of the same impression."

Nichols jerked his head in my direction. "You want to hold him on anything?"

Dawg reached up with his hand and massaged the back of his neck. "Far as I can tell from the initial evidence, it went down about as he said. I'm going to be keeping his weapon for a while, and after the tech guys get through, if they ever show up, I may have some more questions for him." He turned to me now. "You going to be where I can find you easy?"

"Not planning on leaving the area," I said. "Either before sundown or after."

Dawg looked at Nichols. "Wouldn't hurt any to duct tape his mouth, would it?"

Nichols shook his head. "He'd probably find a way to tear it off. Probably take him half a day to figure out how, but he would."

"If you want," Dawg said to me, "you can go ahead and take off. But be handy for either me or the sheriff if we want you. Josh, keep us apprised if anything in the city has to do with this?"

Nichols agreed, and the two of us walked back over to my car.

"You know where Carson is?" I asked.

"Last I knew, he's holding up in his hotel. Even though he'd been MIA for a couple of days, they'd paid for a week in advance. We released him, thanks to that shark attorney of yours, but made it pretty clear we wanted him in the area."

"May want to keep pretty close tabs on him," I said. "In case those two have any friends in the area."

"Way ahead of you, hotshot. I've got a team keeping an eye on him. After all, he's still our best guess for killing Miss Truell. I'm guessing your budding TV career is in the dumper now?"

"Probably. Actually, I think Lisa's more upset about it than I am. She was looking forward to extra publicity for the gym."

Nichols grunted, then started to say something, but before he could my phone chirped.

I gave Nichols a look, and he shrugged.

I pulled the phone out of my pocket.

"Hello."

"They about done with you there?" Lt. Santiago's voice asked. "And whatever you do don't announce who you're talking to."

I glanced around the scene. A van with county markings rocketed its way into the parking lot and screeched to a stop. The county crime scene people had finally shown up.

Three youngsters, almost clones of the EMT's, crawled out of the van, lugging all sorts of packs with them and, without a word to anyone else on the scene, began doing their stuff.

Because most of the area tax base is in Providence, the staff of the various county agencies tend to be younger people barely starting their careers, bagging hours and experience until they can move up the ladder somewhere else.

Between Nichols and his people, the deputies, the EMT's still waiting to haul off the guy I'd shot, and the crime scene guys and gals, plus the onlookers still inside the store peering out through the windows at all the commotion, this little burg was seeing more excitement than it had in who knew how long.

But the one thing I didn't see was anything or anyone who Santiago would want to keep his presence secret from.

"Okay," I said into the phone. "Mum's the word."

"Need to talk."

"Okay."

"Somewhere public where we won't be noticed."

"Public but not noticed?" I queried.

"Yeah. How about the Tonga?"

"If that's your idea of discrete," I told Santiago, "give me about twenty minutes."

"See you then." The lieutenant hung up.

A somewhat client suspected of murder, the local mob interested in my comings and goings, and now the chief detective for the city wanted a private meet.

What more could this week bring?

CHAPTER TWENTY-ONE

T HE TONGA, ONE OF OUR BETTER-KNOWN local coffee shops, at this time of day would be filled almost entirely with college students, mostly young but some verging into middle age.

In other words, almost zero chance Santiago or I would run into anyone we knew.

In another hour things would be different, as folks who work downtown would begin taking off work and stopping by for a little refreshment before heading home, but for a while we were probably safe.

The main question in my mind was safe from what.

Stepping into the Tonga always felt to me like running an obstacle course. They have an assortment of tables, both mid-size and small, scattered about, along with three or four mismatched chairs to go with each table. The line of people waiting to get their coffee, or whatever sugared, caramelled, and cappuccioned up concoction they were drinking, usually cuts right down the middle of the seating area.

The usual bubblings and whirlings, along with the mixed aromas of around thirty different types of drinks, not to mention the combined chattering and clacking of keyboards from all those tables, usually brought me close to sensory overload.

I spotted Santiago sitting at a table with three chairs along the back wall, a cup of something in front of him and, deciding I didn't need to caffeinate or sugar high my system, headed his way.

As I got to the table, he looked up and gave my jeans and tee-shirt a once over.

"You dress worse than most of these students," he said as I sat down.

"At least I dress better than most of their teachers. You're kind of dressing down yourself."

Santiago himself was clothed quite a bit differently than I'd ever seen him. He had on a pair of black slacks that may have cost three or four hundred dollars and tasseled black loafers which probably doubled that in price. All this topped off by a short-sleeved, white shirt that glistened so much I was pretty sure it was pure silk.

No suit. Not even a jacket and tie.

I couldn't remember if I'd ever seen the lieutenant dressed so casually, but I was pretty sure I hadn't. Without long sleeves or a suit coat, the compact musculature of the man jumped out at you.

"Off duty today?" I asked.

Santiago grunted and took a drink from his cup. It looked like he'd gone with straight black coffee.

"A call went out about you a few minutes ago," he said. "You had a bit of trouble outside of town."

"A little bit," I said.

"You put one down, correct?"

"Yeah, but I'm hoping nothing comes of it. Pretty clear-cut self-defense."

Santiago grunted, then took another sip.

I guessed the cop had something to say, and I also guessed it'd be better to let him get to it his own way.

"Assumption being this has something to do with the Truell thing?" Santiago asked.

"Best guess. I don't really have anything else going on at the moment. But why go to the trouble of asking me? They called Nichols out. Will he clue you in?"

He put his cup down and peered at me. "Meaning what?"

"You seem to be out of touch with your office recently. Something going on?"

Santiago leaned back in his chair and gave me his first straight-on look since I'd sat down. "This Truell case. There's an assumption it's more than likely concerned with organized crime in some way."

"That's still only a possibility."

"Didn't you come up with the idea?"

I shrugged. "Based on some stuff Carson gave me. I put two and two together, but the two's were supplied by someone else."

Santiago grunted again and stared off into space for a moment.

"If it's true, there could be some heavy hitters from out west floating into town, if not already here."

"The thought had crossed my mind, especially around the time I was being used as target practice. but I didn't get a chance to question the survivor before the sheriffs showed up," I said.

"Don't worry. If there's anything to get, Nichols will get it out of them."

"They jumped me outside the city limits," I pointed out.

"You know it doesn't matter. For something like this, especially if it seems connected to an ongoing homicide, we're going to be the primaries."

"Okay," I said, "then what am I doing here? Why'd you call me?"

Santiago paused, and for the first time in my memory I caught of hint of hesitation, of uncertainty, in his manner. For a moment, the fingers of his right hand played with his napkin, twisting it back and forth a couple of different ways before smoothing it back out again.

The cop looked back up at me. "I'm going to be on the sidelines for a while," he said.

I nodded, almost as if I had half a clue what he was talking about.

"Why?" I asked.

"Personal reasons. Call it a leave of absence. Nichols will be running the squad, including the Truell case."

I nodded again, though probably not as convincingly as the first time. "Is this leave of yours planned ahead of time?"

His lips quirked. "Depends on who could do the planning."

I didn't have the faintest idea what he meant by that. "So why tell me?" I asked.

"Just wanted to let you know if you need anything on this, Nichols is the one to go to."

I thought about pointing out I usually went to Josh first anyway but decided not to.

Santiago stood up, pulled a money clip out of his pocket, and while I was trying to figure out the last time I'd ever seen anyone using a money clip, threw a couple of bills on the table.

"You need any help on whatever this is?" I asked.

The cop shook his head. "Like I said, wanted to let you know Nichols is the go-to man now."

"Uh huh."

"Take care of yourself, Quinton," he said before turning and walking out.

CHAPTER TWENTY-TWO

I GAVE IT ABOUT FIVE MINUTES AFTER Santiago left the Tonga before I called Nichols on his cell. He must have returned to the station because I could hear the faint murmur of squad room activity in the background.

"Can you talk?" were my first words to him.

"Hold on." A moment later, the background murmur cut off. "Okay. Had to step into the lieutenant's office for some privacy. What's up?"

"You tell me. What's going on with your boss?"

"Meaning what?"

"Knock it off, Josh. I was just with Santiago. He made it sound like they've got him half out the door. Want to fill me in?"

Over the phone, Nichols sigh sounded like a waterfall. "Might was well. As many cops as work out at your gym, you'll hear bits and pieces of it sooner or later."

"So give me the whole scoop."

"He's on an unofficial suspension."

"Unofficial suspension? Is that even a real thing?"

"It wasn't until about a day ago," Nichols said.

"Hate to tell you this, Josh, but you're not making a whole lot of sense right now."

Nichols put out another sigh, longer and deeper this time, and I could visualize his shoulders slumping.

"It's like this," he said, "a month ago, we had a fairly decent drug bust at Jackson High School."

"I think I heard about that on the news."

"Probably did," Santiago said. "Rounded up about twenty users, holders, and dealers. All but a couple of them young enough that, at least for now, we had to keep their names out of the media."

"Okay," I said, not sure I liked where this was going.

"One of the names we suppressed was Troy Farrell, sixteen years old."

I waited.

"You know the kind of kids who go to Jackson," Santiago said.

"In general, those whose parents have some influence."

"Right. And they don't get much more influential than Mark Farrell."

"Christ," I said, "the city councilman."

"You got it," Nichols said. "Ordinarily, it wouldn't matter how much parents kick and scream, and believe me the Farrells did a lot, we were going by the book."

"Including the DA's office?" I asked.

Nichols paused for a fraction of a second before continuing. "So far. But we're still in the middle of the process and DA's a political animal so, . . ."

"So Farrell's put a target on Santiago's back," I said. "Because of the kid?"

"That plus he's still fairly tight with Bob Marlowe."

I could see why Nichols had gone into the inner office before having this talk. "The mayor's pretty much out of the picture these days, isn't he?" I asked.

"Sure," Nichols said. "But just because he decided not to run for reelection doesn't mean he doesn't have some friends. And Farrell's one of them. Couple that with his kid being caught in our roundup, and he's got it out for the whole department."

"I'm still not seeing how this leads to Santiago being given a shove," I said.

Nichols took a long, deep breath, then slowly let it out. "We have the possibility, no matter how faint, the Truell killing may have org crime connections . . ."

"A possibility you only got because I suggested it."

"Doesn't matter where it came from, the point is . . ."

"Christ," I said, "the point is Santiago's got a perfect storm coming down on him."

"You got it," Nichols said.

I skulled it over for a moment. "There's been questions about him since he came to town," I said.

"Yep. How's he afford his lifestyle. How does a cop, no matter the rank, manage to drive around in a new Porsche every year. What happened to make him leave a promising career in Chicago. Stuff like that."

"And if someone, say some friend of the good mayor's, has been waiting for him to stub his toe . . ."

"It's a mixture almost too perfect for Farrell to pass up," Nichols said.

"They going to fire him?"

"Not sure," Nichols said. "Way I get it, for now he's on a really short leash until he can alleviate their concerns."

"Alleviate."

"Yep."

"So what exactly does short leash mean?"

"Means unless he can prove he's got no connection to any type of corruption, he's one foot out the door."

Nichols didn't bring it up, but I was remembering a time not too long ago when he himself had been in something of a similar predicament. "Anything I can do to help him?" I asked.

"Far as I can see, the easiest thing all around would be to get to the bottom of the Truell thing. That was the final straw. Farrell and one or two of his buddies are taking two unconnected things and making it look like Santiago's some sort of Mafia cop. Thing is, even without any direct correlation between the lieutenant and the boys, merely the idea there's some sort of operation going on in town, when you combine it with Santiago's fairly questionable past, is enough to give the town council a case of hives."

"Where's your chief sit on this?" I asked.

"Chief would like to help. Hell, he's the one who brought the lieutenant out to our little paradise here. But it's an election year, and even if his job isn't a strictly political one . . ."

"Yeah," I said. "I've got it. If it helps, I think I can safely say that the actual mob wasn't involved."

"I'm guessing I don't want to hear about how you're so sure," Nichols replied.

"And if it turns out he gets cleared on any sort of involvement in anything?"

"Then I guess things go back to normal," Nichols said, "until the next time he gets crosswise of a council person."

"In other words," I said, "one step at a time."

"Pretty much."

CHAPTER TWENTY-THREE

So now, I had a couple of things on my plate.. Three if you counted not feeling particularly safe and secure after a couple of out-of-town gunners had taken a run at me.

After hanging up from Nichols, I decided it was time for another talk with Carson. I had originally thought I was out of all this once I'd turned him over to the cops and got Bernie Lyman to represent him. But between being waylaid on a county road by some hoods and hearing about Santiago's troubles, it was time to take a slightly more active role in the whole thing.

The attack would have been enough by itself. When someone tries to do you in, it's best to find out who and why. Santiago's problem added another layer to it.

The lieutenant and I weren't friends, and it would be a stretch to even call us colleagues. More like lukewarm acquaintances. But we got along better lately than we had when he first showed up in town, and he'd proven himself to be a pretty decent cop, even with all the mystery about how he supported his lifestyle, and I didn't much care for the idea of a blowhard on the city council making life difficult for him.

It was clearly a case of some of his political enemies waiting for a time to strike and deciding now was it. And since the whole thing had blown up with the murder of Wendy Truell, I figured it wouldn't hurt to poke around a bit and see what I could turn up.

My first stop was my apartment. Even though Deputy Dawg had taken my weapon for his investigation, a normal part of procedure, with some strangers gunning for me I didn't want to be walking around unarmed. Therefore, a quick stop home to pick up a secondary piece I keep on hand, and I was back on the road.

I headed over to Carson's hotel. It was time for him and I to have a much more serious talk than we'd had to date.

True to Nichols's word, I found him tucked away in his room. I also spotted the team of two detectives, one in the lobby and one in the hallway, keeping an eye on him, but I probably wouldn't have noticed them if I hadn't known they were there already.

"Come on in," Carson said as he opened the door to me. "I was wondering when you'd show up."

I followed him into a suite that, at least as far as floor plan, looked a lot like Wendy Truell's one floor above. The couch was a light tan leather instead of black. The 50-inch TV was in its own entertainment center, rather than bracketed to the wall as in Wendy's room, and the guest desk was in a different location.

Other than that, in basic layout the two suites were carbon copies.

The big difference, though, was a faint tinge of sloppiness hanging over the whole suite.

Where Wendy's rooms had been pristine, if one had ignored the sight of her corpse and the bloody couch cushions, Carson's suite looked a lot sloppier even with the absence of a dead body.

A couple of shirts were thrown over the back of one of the chairs; a few fast-food containers, including one from a taco shop down the street, perched on the corner desk; and an assortment of used glasses decorated the coffee table in front of the couch.

"Can I get you something?" Carson asked, angling over towards a room service cart in the corner next to the desk.

"No," I said. "We need to talk, John."

He stopped and turned back. For the first time, he got a good look at me, and I guess what he saw in my face made him sober up a bit.

"What's up, Sam?"

I sat down on the couch without asking, and after a moment, he sat down in one of the easy chairs. "Two gunners tried to take me out a couple of hours ago," I said.

Carson nodded.

"The cops haven't ID'd them yet," I continued, "but the best guess is they're from out of town."

Another nod, still no comment, and his eyes began to look a little unfocused.

"So the working theory, naturally, is they've got something to do with Wendy's murder."

"Was there gunfire?" Carson asked.

"Shooting? Yeah. That's what I meant by tried to take me out. I had to put one of them down."

"You mean kill him?" Carson asked.

"That's what put down usually means, John."

His look became even vaguer, as if he was half watching and listening to me and half looking off into space. "What about the other one? Did he get away or did you have to draw on him too?"

"That's not the point, John. What I'm saying is . . ."

"I mean, we'd have to simulate it, of course, but it would make a great scene in the series. You know, lone hero facing off against imported hitmen."

I sighed. I would have shaken my head at the same time, but I suddenly didn't have the energy for two moves at once. "John, this isn't TV. This is real life. Those two were somehow connected to your problems."

"I know it's real, Sam. I'm not a complete idiot. I'm thinking ahead here."

"Try thinking in the here and now instead," I said. "If somebody's coming after me, they're probably looking for you as well."

He came a little into focus then. "Me?"

"Of course you."

"Why would anyone want to do me in?" he asked.

"Well, someone did kill your partner a few days ago," I said.

"And you think the same high-powered international hitter who came after Wendy wants to the same to me?"

"John, for one there's no indication the killer was international. For two, if you keep talking that way the courts are going to throw you in the clink on general principles."

"But even if her murder is somehow connected with the business, Wendy was the one who handled all the books and everything. I'm just the . . ."

"Yeah, yeah, the creative end," I said. "Tell me, John. Do you have any way of knowing, for sure, not guessing or hoping, that Wendy was involved with criminals?"

"Doesn't it seem kind of obvious?" he asked. "After all, you gave me the idea."

I didn't want to mention yet my visit from O'Flaherty. I needed to pull as much as I could out of Carson's own experience, and I didn't want any of that cluttered up with more of his imagination. "I know. But the cops and courts generally like proof of some kind. Not just assumptions, which is all we've got at the moment."

Something came over Carson's expression. It was little more than a flicker, something close to confusion, or maybe indecision, and not for the first time in dealing with the man I wondered if he was being anywhere near straight with me.

I wondered if I should try really stripping things away and address him by his real name of Sammy Lemwitz.

"What would help?" he asked.

"I don't know. Did you ever, in hindsight, ever meet any of these supposed underworld figures?"

"Nope. Like I keep telling you, man, Wendy handled all the business stuff. I kept as far from that as I could get."

A new stray thought occurred to me. "Is there any way she could have been playing some sort of double game? Working something else on her own?"

Carson's face did the scrunch thing. "You mean like undercutting them? Not being straight as far as their cut?"

"Assuming any of this is remotely factual," I said, "yeah."

"Could be," Carson said. "After all, when you're talking goombahs, I'm not sure they'd understand the distinction in some sort of organizational chart."

I could have pointed out to him a lot of mob and cartel figures, at least at the higher levels, while not necessarily Mensa candidates were about as crafty as they came concerning business.

I'd met one or two over the years who could give most Fortune 500 CEO's a run for their money in terms of business and finance. But because I had a hunch no matter how I explained it I'd be bumping up against Carson's fantasy world, I let it go.

"What about the legit side?" I asked.

"Huh?"

"I mean the actual company, Monumental Productions. What are your exact titles?"

"Oh, well, Wendy was down as the president, and I'm Executive VP in Charge of Programming."

I pondered that for a few minutes while Carson fidgeted in his chair.

"Any other executives?" I finally asked.

"Sure. A couple more VP's, some department heads and such."

"Have you talked to them yet?" I asked.

"Talked to them?"

"About Wendy's death?"

"Not exactly, Sam. I mean, the cops have been carrying on and everything, and considering who all she was involved with, I figured just as well to lie low until I got the all clear."

"Christ!" I said as I jumped up from the couch and pulled out my phone.

"Josh," I said when Nichols answered. "There's other officers in Monumental. All of them back in California." I looked at Carson, who nodded in agreement. "Carson hasn't talked to them yet. They may not know about Wendy's death."

"Really?" Nichols said. "Too bad we didn't think to check on the company as part of our investigation, huh?"

I grimaced, impressed beyond description by my own naivete. "I guess that would have been obvious to do, wouldn't it?"

"It would. For what it's worth, as far as we can tell the other officers in the corporation are fairly clean, at least by Hollywood standards."

"You got names and such?" I asked.

"Yeah. Gimme a minute and let me get my notes."

A lot of people would have expected the sergeant to call his report up on a computer screen or some such. But I knew that, despite all the high-tech gadgets that make up the modern police vehicle, even the rookiest of rookies still keep old-fashioned spiral pocket notebooks to record initial information.

"Okay," Nichols said, "here we go. There's a Janice Manson, forty-six years old, who's their main contract supervisor."

"Which means what?" I asked.

"From what I can gather, she makes sure the bills are paid on time and all the contracts are signed."

"Okay."

"A guy named Fred Freiburger, fifty-two, who's down as the logistics head. Means he coordinates all the day workers, production schedules, and permits for them."

"Uh huh."

"Finally, there's some dude named Sid Weintropf. He's down as their mobile integration coordinator, whatever the heck that is."

I thought about it for a minute. "Almost sounds like corporate speak for a chauffeur," I said.

"Hmm, you may be right at that. Any rate, those are the three other officers of the company."

"What about possible danger to them?"

If I'd closed my eyes, I could have visualized Nichols shrugging before answering. "We did what we could. Made it clear to them as much as we knew what had happened to her. Called up the force in Fresno. You do know you're big show biz wheeler and dealer buddy has his offices in Fresno?"

"Yeah," I said, "I knew that."

"Well anyway, called the Fresno cops and explained the situation. It's a little tricky because the whole damned Southern California scene is a patchwork of communities, kind of like Kansas City but on a much more massive scale. One of those folks lives in Malibu, another in Oxnard, and the third in a town called West Covina, wherever the heck that is."

"So it's pretty much up to the locals down there to sort it all out on their end?" I asked.

"Yep. For what it's worth, the suggestion has also been passed along they hire private security, which will probably do about as much good as anything."

"Good enough," I said. "One other thing, though. After what happened to me today, don't you think we need more than two of your people keeping an eye on Carson?"

Before Nichols could answer, someone knocked on the door.

Carson got up to answer it, but I grabbed his arm and held him in place.

"You expecting anyone?" I whispered to him.

Carson shook his head. "Huh uh. It's probably one of the cops outside needing to take a leak or something."

The knock came again, a little more insistent this time.

"I don't think so," I said. "They'd announce themselves."

"Josh," I said into the phone. "Check in with your officers you've got watching Carson, then you'd better get some people down here real quick."

"What's up?" Nichols asked.

A third knock, louder by far than the first two. And still no one identifying themselves on the other side.

"Not sure," I told Nichols. "But I think something's about to go down. Get on it."

I ended the call, threw my phone onto the couch, and shoved Carson halfway across the room.

I barely managed to crouch down on the far end of the couch, my gun drawn, before the door flung open and three guys came charging in, weapons drawn.

CHAPTER TWENTY-FOUR

DEPENDING ON HOW YOU LOOK AT it, Providence is either a small city or a large town. Either way, we have our fair share of violent crime, especially in the last ten years or so, but we're not exactly a hotbed of depravity and running gun battles. If the average metropolitan cop in the United States goes their entire career without even drawing their gun from its holster, that probably goes double for a Providence cop.

So being the focus of hostile guns twice in one day was stretching it, and by this point I was getting a little damned tired of it.

I didn't know what had happened to the two cops guarding Carson, but pretty obviously nothing good considering three gunsels had shown up at his door.

At the moment I wasn't too sure exactly what to do about it.

Duke Prowder, my old St. Louis mentor in the PI game, had trained me as well as he could in all the various aspects of the business, which made me fairly competent in some areas, pretty good in others.

For instance, I'm not bad at tailing someone in a car, at least as long as the traffic's pretty heavy, not all that good at picking a lock, especially since that's kind of frowned on as illegal.

I'm also fairly confident when it comes to the physical end of things, even though it's become obvious in the last few years I'm edging past my prime, but facing down three gunners at one time, in a confined room, is a bit beyond my skill set.

Though at the moment I had little choice in the matter.

The three came in one after the other, splitting both left and right to divide themselves as targets. A small part of me wondered how they'd managed to get through the locked door, but at the moment that was the least of my worries.

They were in, and I had to do something about it.

I reared up from the end of the couch and snapped a shot at the guy in front, a tall, skinny red-headed dude. I was aiming for his mass, but he ducked at the last instant, and I got him in the shoulder.

He spun to the side and down, leaving a clear field of fire for the other two. One, a short Hispanic, veered to the left and went for Carson while the other, another short guy, white this time, drew a bead on me.

I popped down behind the couch just as he fired, and his bullet went over my head and into the wall behind me. To the side, I heard Carson scream but at the moment couldn't do much for him.

I shifted about six inches to the side and took a quick peek. The Latin dude had settled into a traditional shooter's stance, legs shifted in a straddle and his free hand supporting the wrist of his gun hand. I angled my weapon to the side of the couch and upwards, trying to get the best possible shot I could, but in the split second before I fired three more men, all wearing navy blue windbreakers, appeared in the room through the still open door.

"Freeze!" one of them yelled. My attacker whirled, his weapon still extended, and before I could blink, one of the blue windbreakers drilled him right through the chest.

The guy in front of me dropped, and the three new intruders, as one, whirled to the side where Carson was flat on his back and the remaining attacker stood over him.

That guy glanced behind his shoulder, saw the array of men with weapons in front of him, not to mention one buddy dead on the floor and the other angled against the wall nursing a bleeding shoulder, and took the wiser course of action.

He dropped his weapon and raised his hands as high as he could.

To the side, John Carson whimpered a little.

Two of the windbreaker guys rushed over to the man standing over Carson, threw him to the floor, and yanked his arms behind his back.

By this point, my brain had managed to catch up enough I didn't need the three initials, F.B.I, lettered on the backs of their jackets to tell me the stakes for everyone had just raised up quite a bit.

CHAPTER TWENTY-FIVE

"**E**XACTLY HOW IS THIS GUY INVOLVED in all this?" Special Agent Phil Hendricks asked, pointing to me.

We were corralled in Santiago's office: myself, Josh Nichols, Hendricks and the other two FBI guys who'd burst into Carson's hotel room.

Carson himself was down in a holding cell on the ground floor. Not booked for anything, but considering the recent attempt on his life, it seemed fairly necessary to keep him under lock and key for a while, at least until someone figured out what to do with him.

One good thing about the multiple gunfights that afternoon. I seriously doubted anyone was still looking at Carson for Wendy Truell's murder.

Although there were plenty of chairs around to accommodate, at the moment everyone was standing in a kind of ragged circle staring each other down.

"Mr. Quinton is a private investigator here in Providence," Nichols said in a calm, controlled tone.

"I know that," Hendricks shot back. "What I want to know is why he's messing around in a murder case? Tell me that, huh, Sergeant."

Hendricks was a lean man, even in the blue windbreaker that looked a little silly on a mild September evening. He had a solid, if not overdeveloped musculature and an almost ruler-straight posture, and I guessed somewhere in his background lurked some military service. With his brown hair and eyes, he wore what seemed to be a permanent scowl.

"I'm going to follow procedure, if you don't mind," Nichols said, his tone making it clear to everyone how annoyed he was.

I thought about sticking my tongue out at Hendricks, but figured the fed wouldn't quite see it as a mark of my professionalism.

"To begin with," Nichols resumed in the face of Hendricks's continued scowling, "Mr. Quinton has a personal relationship with the people involved."

"Relationship?" Hendricks asked.

I took that as my cue and filled the feds in on my interactions with Carson and Truell.

"So he was going to make you some sort of TV star?" Hendricks asked me.

"It never got as far as anything concrete," I said. "Actually, I got the feeling the whole thing was a wild notion of Carson's."

"Wild enough to have him and his partner fly all the way out here to discuss it?"

"Yeah," I said. "That part doesn't quite make sense to me."

"Maybe it does," Hendricks said, and one of his two sidebars nodded.

Nichols and I looked at each other, and when it appeared Hendricks wasn't going to explain his remark, Nichols continued.

"Now that you're up to speed on Mr. Quinton's involvement, suppose you tell us what you're doing here in our fair city. You from the Kansas City office?"

"St. Louis, actually."

"Six of one," Nichols said. "What brings you out here?"

Hendricks started staring at me again.

I wondered if he'd feel better if I started knocking my knees together.

After he probably felt as if he'd milked the moment for all he could, the fed spoke up. "This is clearly a federal matter, Sergeant. I don't care about any sort of relationship. I don't think Mr. Quinton belongs in this conversation."

"This is also a Providence police matter, agent. Maybe I want him here."

"Staking out your territory, Sergeant? You should be careful. Way I hear it, going off halfcocked didn't turn out too well for your lieutenant back in his former department."

If the dig bothered Nichols, he didn't show it much. I saw maybe a slight tightening of his jaw muscles but no other reaction.

"Far as that goes," Hendricks continued as he glanced at me, "from what I understand Mr. Quinton here has been known to occasionally associate with known felons in your town."

"I don't know about any felons as in plural," I said, "but if you meant to speak in the singular that would be Sean O'Flaherty you're referring to?"

"You'd better believe it, bub. No one who has anything to do with that cocksucker can be entirely clean."

"While you're at it, don't forget the late, unlamented Paddy O' Brien," I said.

Hendricks started to say something else, but before he could Nichols spoke up.

"We're not here to talk ancient history, Agent Hendricks," he said. "Mr. Quinton's involved in this mess, whatever it is. So either you start talking or get the hell out of this office and we'll handle things ourselves."

Amazingly, Hendricks began glowering even more, something I hadn't thought possible. His eyes narrowed to slits, and the red in his neck and face made me worry about his blood pressure.

He probably wasn't used to being spoken to that way, especially not by a local cop. But as far as I could see, all the crimes committed thus far had been at the state level, leaving me wondering exactly why the hell the feds were mixing in this at all.

After a few moments, Hendricks shook his head and snagged one of the chairs in front of Santiago's desk.

"What the hell," he said to the entire room, "the damned thing's pretty much blown up in our face anyway." He half swiveled to look at me. "Don't quit your day job, hotshot. You were about to throw in with the wrong crowd."

"How so?" I asked, doing my best to act the part of the dumb hick.

Hendricks scowled some more, exchanging fierce looks with his colleagues, before turning back to Nichols.

"Is John Carson your main suspect in the Truell killing?" he asked.

"At the moment," Nichols said, "though officially there's not even enough evidence to call him a suspect."

"You may want to broaden your net a bit."

"Meaning?"

Instead of answering directly, Henricks looked my way again. "This man's a civilian. He doesn't belong in here."

"Look," Nichols said, his face tightening again, "whatever big bad secret you're working on that brought you to our town here, I'm guessing it's been blown apart, otherwise you wouldn't have been staking out that hotel. How about we cut the Roy Ranger Secret Agent crap and get down to whatever you have to say."

Hendricks spent another few minutes scowling and harrumphing until he finally sank all the way back in his chair.

"Monumental Productions," Hendricks said, "is nothing but a shill company. It's a money laundering tool for some of the drug cartels, biker gangs, and assorted crime families back west."

"We kind of had that figured out," Nichols said.

"You knew . . ." For once, Hendricks looked a little put out.

"Not exactly knew, but it was a theory we were working on."

"I wasn't entirely believing it," I said. "Carson's not exactly the most stable person when it comes to reality, and I thought maybe he was coming up with some wild story to get himself off the hook for her murder."

"Yeah," Hendricks said. "I hear the guy comes up with stories a lot."

"But with two shootouts in one day," I said, "plus your say so, I guess the guy was telling the truth."

"As much as he knew."

Nichols and I leaned forward a little.

"There's more?" Nichols asked.

Hendricks would never make it as a poker player. I sat there watching his face contort as he struggled with deciding something. His shoulders tensed up, and for a second I thought he was going to get up and storm out of the office, taking his ball and going home.

Instead, after several seconds, he must have decided to play. "What the hell? Like you said, it's all kind of shot now."

"What is?" Nichols asked.

"Wendy Truell reached out to us a couple of months ago."

"Reached out?"

Hendricks nodded. "For some reason, she'd decided she'd had enough, and she was willing to work with us."

"Work with you," I said, "as in witness protection?"

Hendricks nodded. "She was going to give us the goods on all of her clients in return for a fresh start somewhere else."

"I know I'm just a small-town cop," Nichols said, "but I was always under the impression it was the marshals who handle the Witness Protection end of things."

Hendricks nodded. "They do, after the Bureau gets whatever we can out of them to make cases. Marshals just handle the protection end of things once the hard work's over with."

"Shit," Nichols said. "Where and when was all the cooperation supposed to take place?"

"Where and when do you think?" Hendricks asked.

"That's why she came out here with Carson," I said. "This was the meeting place to get her away from home turf so she'd have a better chance of cutting loose."

Hendricks nodded. "And now it's all blown to hell."

CHAPTER TWENTY-SIX

TWENTY MINUTES LATER, I WAITED OUT front of the station for Carson to walk out. He blinked at the streetlights, as if he'd been in stir for a decade instead of an hour, took one look at me and turned to walk the other way.

If you squinted real hard, you could almost see the target on his back.

I started after him, not exactly running but keeping to more of a dignified lope, and considering I was several inches taller it took me all of eight feet to catch up.

When I grasped him by the elbow, he sighed and slumped his shoulders. "Keep away from me."

"Don't think so, John. We need to talk."

"All I want to talk about is the quickest way to get out of this hick 'burg and back to some place civilized."

"Like L.A.?" I asked.

"Don't knock it, big guy. At least out there someone's not waiting around every corner to shoot you down."

"You sure we're talking about the same Los Angeles?"

"You know what I mean."

"I'm not sure you do. If you're really this scared, why are you headed back to your hotel?"

Carson's face scrunched up a bit in thought. "Where am I supposed to go?"

"With me," I said. "Until we can figure out what to do with you."

The face scrunch continued. "I don't get it. I thought the cops weren't looking at me anymore."

"Nichols and his squad have pretty much written you off as a suspect, considering what's happened the last several hours, but the feds are still interested in you."

Carson glanced over his shoulder back at the station several feet away. "Then why did they let me go?"

I grinned, gripped his arm even tighter, and began walking him down the sidewalk. "Because local cops don't care much for feds, and my guess would be right about now Nichols is telling them you've been sprung. Besides, you were the intended victim in this, not the perpetrator."

Carson turned back to look at me. "Is there something that's happened I don't know about? I'm not a complete idiot, Sam. Why the sudden lack of interest in me?"

I thought about it for a moment. Although it was heavy stuff, no one had exactly sworn me to secrecy, and as Hendricks had said the whole thing was probably a moot point after Wendy's death, and if her killer or killers was ever put on trial, the story would come out anyway.

Plus, it did concern him directly, and whether the feds would end up agreeing or not, the man had a right to know why people were shooting at him.

Beyond that, I hadn't taken a blood oath of secrecy or anything like that. If Special Agent Hendricks had overlooked taping my mouth shut, that was on him.

"Let's find somewhere to park it, John," I said. "We've got a lot to talk about."

CHAPTER TWENTY-SEVEN

"**S**HE WAS GOING TO DO WHAT?" Carson asked me a couple of minutes later.

We'd settled into a booth in one of the handful of bars that populate Main Street. In the time I'd been in town, this one had started as a sports bar, then transformed into a piano bar, before evolving into a comedy club for a year before settling into just plain bar. The drinks weren't all that great, and they definitely weren't cheap, but the lighting was dim, and with most people still out to dinner hardly anyone was in there.

Considering the price of the drinks in the place, plus the fact I was paying, we'd both settled on beer.

"Throw in with the feds," I repeated. "Turn informer on them for a shot at a new, clean life somewhere else."

Carson twisted and turned his mug on the table a couple of times. "Geez," he said. "You talking that witness protection bullshit? Like at the end of *Goodfellas*?"

"That's about it," I said. "According to them, she'd been keeping meticulous records on all of her—I guess clients—for several years. She was willing to turn all of it over to the feds for a second shot somewhere else."

"Who are they?"

"Who are who?" I asked.

"The people she was working for. Was it the mob?"

I shook my head and took a drink before answering. "Not mob

in the way you're probably thinking. Obviously, the feds didn't share a whole lot of info there. But they let out that she was working with several smaller scale drug cartels, plus a few assorted hangers on."

Carson frowned down at the table for a minute. "I didn't know anything about that."

"I kind of figured not," I said. I left it at that, not adding that if she was keeping the money laundering from him, she sure wouldn't divulge her plans to split. Plus, if I had something I wanted to keep secret, the last person I'd confide in would be John Carson.

Carson fidgeted in his seat. For a moment, I thought he was going to get up and start pacing, but after a few seconds he settled down a bit.

"You think you know someone," he said. "You work with them for years, build up a body of collaboration, then you find this out."

"Got to ask you a question, John. And I don't know a polite way of going about it."

He took in some air, held it for a beat, then exhaled. "Go ahead."

"How much did you know about your business?" I asked. "I mean the real nuts and bolts of it. Don't give me any BS about the land of creativity. How much about the actual business did you know?"

Taking another deep breath, he put his hands on the table in front of us, palms down, and did a little faux pushup.

After he relaxed from the move, he looked up at me. "Well, I guess it's pretty obvious I didn't know too much."

"So when you say Wendy ran day-to-day operations, you mean it."

"Of course. Hell, most of the time I was only in the office once a week, if that."

"Wining and dining creative people the rest of the time?" Christ, I'd been around the guy long enough I was even starting to talk like him.

Carson grinned at me, and I thought I could see a little heartbreak in his eyes. "Not really. I'd say about half the time I was zonked at home in front of the TV, waiting for the phone to ring."

"And meanwhile Wendy was running the show."

"What can I say," Carson's grin widened, though it looked a bit tired to me, "she's the one with the head for figures."

"Was," I said.

"Huh?"

"She was the one with the head for figures. She's dead, remember?"

The smirk vanished, and Carson's shoulders drooped. I gave him a moment of silence. "Yeah, I guess that is the right way to phrase it," he said after a few minutes.

We sat there for a while and drank. Two men whiling away the evening.

"I guess I should head back home now, huh?" Carson said after draining half his mug.

I frowned at him. "Why do you say that?"

"Well, hell. If Wendy was pulling a double cross on some greaser type gangsters, sounds like I'm off the hook, right?"

"John," I said, "look at me."

For the first time since we'd sat down, he gave me a straight-on look.

"You need to realize exactly what's going on here," I said. "The fact Wendy was pulling some shenanigans doesn't get you off. If anything, you're in deeper than you were."

"How's that? Now that the feds are mixed in . . ."

"The feds are 'mixed in' as you put it because they just lost their golden goose. With Wendy dead, they've lost the big bonanza they were counting on."

"Right. Like I said, off the hook."

"And since they don't have Wendy, they're probably going to come for you."

Carson gulped and did a little half fling against the back of the booth. "Me?"

"You," I said.

"But I don't know anything about any money laundering.. That was all Wendy."

"You're a partner in the business," I pointed out. "And you knew enough to be suspecting something going on for a while whether you wanted to admit it to yourself or not."

"Well, yeah, but how many times do I have to say I was only working the creative end? Wendy did all the books."

"You don't have to tell me about it. I understood from the beginning."

"Then what . . ."

"But you're probably going to have to tell the feds over and over. Even then, they might not believe you."

"Now hold on there, Sam." By this point, the poor guy had pushed himself far enough back he was about to merge into the back of the booth. "You saying they're going to expect me to give up all kinds of gangland info?"

"It's what I'd expect if I was in their shoes," I said. "In which case, it helps that I got you a good lawyer the other day."

Carson wiped his hand across his forehead. "Geez, what a mess."

"And there's more," I said.

"More?" The word came out as a croak. "What more could there be?"

"The boys."

"Who?"

"All of Wendy's various clients. You know, the ones whose money she was handling."

Carson's face whitened by about three shades. "You saying they're going to come after me? But I don't know anything about it."

"You keep saying that," I said, "but they don't know that. And if you didn't notice a few hours ago in your hotel room, someone's already coming after you."

The guy actually began to tremble right there in front of me. "You've got to help me get out of this, Sam. You've got to do something here."

I shook my head. "This is way out of my level of expertise, John. The best thing you can do is throw yourself at the feds and hope they'll protect you."

"You said a minute ago I was clear." His voice cracked a bit on the last word.

I've seen a lot of scared men before, but I thought Carson was going to shake himself apart.

"Clear in terms of Wendy's murder," I said. "But you're still mixed up in the whole mess. No way around that."

He was gripping the table hard enough I wouldn't have been surprised to see him crack it. "But I've got nothing to give them! You think the government's going to step up and take care of my problems out of the goodness of their heart? They're going to want something out of me, and I've got nothing to give!"

I'd pushed Carson about as far as he would go. It had been a little cruel on my part, but I'd needed to see if he was telling the truth about his ignorance about Wendy's activities, and as far as I could tell, he had been.

Which only left the matter of what to do with him because everything I'd laid out had been absolute truth. The guy was in a mess and, if I could believe him, with no easy way out.

"You've got to help me, Sam. All this stuff is your field, not mine. All I know how to do is produce TV shows. And hell, I'm not all that great even at that. I don't know how to navigate this kind of crap."

I sighed.

"I'll give you whatever you want," Carson continued. "We'll do the show like I said. Only I'll make it real quality, not like my other stuff, and we won't do any of those suggestions you didn't like. Just get me the hell out of this."

I took a deep breath and let it out slowly. "Carson, at the moment the last thing I want is to be involved with you in any kind of business deal. But you are in a jam here, and it's the kind of jam I can help you with. How about we forget all the BS about Hollywood and reality shows and all that, and I'll take you on as a client."

A little color came back into his face. "Cool, man. Thanks. By the way, what uh, what do you charge?"

I quoted him my usual rate. He blinked a couple of times.

"You good for it?" I asked.

He bobbled his head up and down. "Absolutely. No problem, I can make that easy. So what's our first step?"

I was already starting to rethink this.

CHAPTER TWENTY-EIGHT

"**Y**OU LEFT HIM AT HIS HOTEL?" Talia asked me.

It was about an hour later, past ten o'clock. Although Talia usually goes to bed around eleven or so, I'd called ahead of time just to make sure she was still up and if she minded company.

Said I'd had something I had to go over with her.

"You know the answer to that," she'd replied. "You don't need to ask in advance to come over here."

She'd greeted me at the door in a royal blue silk robe, her hair down and makeup-free, with a cup of coffee in each hand. I'd taken the one she offered gratefully, and when we sat down on the sofa she tucked her feet up under her and curled herself into my arms.

I then filled her in on what had gone down all day.

"Two shoot outs in one day?" she'd asked. "And you came out of them without a nick?"

"Only to my nerves," I said. "I'd be glad to go another week without hearing gunfire again."

At which point she'd asked about me leaving Carson alone at his hotel.

"Not hardly," I said. "First, we moved him out of the Trithorn and over to the Radisson out east."

"And the F.B.I just let you take him?"

I smiled. "There was a bit of a lull spot between when the cops let him go and when they told Hendricks they'd done so."

"Because?"

"Because Hendricks came on the scene like General Jackboot, and Nichols took a dislike to him."

Talia shook her head. "I know Josh," she said. "He's too professional to let personal feelings make him screw up."

"True," I said, "but I think he also didn't entirely believe everything Hendricks was laying out. Besides, Nichols had nothing to hold him on, and the feds didn't have a warrant of any kind, meaning nothing really to do but turn him loose."

Talia frowned, and I could almost see the gears working in her brain.

"I know you're the detective," she said, "and I'm just a boring academic, but won't it be pretty easy for the government to track him down? Or to track you for that matter? Can't they just lock on your cell phones or some such?"

Now I didn't just smile, I beamed. "They probably could if I hadn't have stopped by a drugstore and bought a couple of new throwaway phones. If they're trying to track me, they'll be staked out in front of The Blaster, which is where I left my regular phone in the desk in my office. Carson's original phone is, last I knew, in a trash basket on Ninth Street."

"But they know where you live and work. They could just trail you, right?"

"They could, but I'm keeping an eye open, and actually I think they've got more problems at the moment than keeping every little eye on me."

"Such as?"

"Well, I'm guessing right about now they're tearing through the physical offices back in California and siccing their forensic accounting people on the company's books, but while they're no doubt looking at the other company officers, Carson's their best bet to get them close to Wendy's records."

"Because as far as we know he's the only one some gangsters are trying to kill?"

"Well, him and me. Don't forgot about me."

"Never," Talia whispered as she snuggled even tighter into me, something I wouldn't have thought possible. "All that makes my day of meetings, conferences, and budgets look tame by comparison. Anything else happen today big fella?"

"Actually, yeah. All that isn't the main reason I came over."

She sat up a bit and did a half twist to look me in the eye. "Really? There's something else?"

I nodded and proceeded to fill her in on Santiago's problem. She listened all the way through, and when I finished, as she often did, she got straight to the heart of what was bothering me.

"Was he asking you for help?"

I thought about it, for about the fiftieth time in the last six hours. "I'm not sure. He's kind of hard to read."

"He asked you for help once before."

"Yep, on the Mosby case. The same thing that's supposedly jamming him up all over again. But back then he came right out and said it, even hired me and agreed to my usual rate. This time he didn't. He was more letting me know why he wouldn't be around for a while."

Talia shook her head, collapsed back on the couch, and gave me a frown.

"What?" I asked.

"Men. You're so goddamned opaque to each other and transparent to the rest of us."

"Meaning?"

"Meaning what would he gain by specifically telling you why he wouldn't be around the office? Wouldn't you figure that out by yourself pretty damned quick?"

"I guess," I said.

"Of course you would. What's more, far as that goes what difference would it make to you?"

"You're saying he was asking me without really asking."

She shook her head again, more violently than before. "Of course, that's what he was doing. But you're both such damned macho guys, not only did you not pick it up, I'd be willing to guess Santiago's not even aware himself that's what he was doing."

"If you're right, what could he be wanting me to do? If I start trying to poke around in a political case like this, I won't get anywhere."

"How do you know if you don't give it a shot?"

I leaned farther back into the couch while I thought that one through. The more I thought about it, the more it felt unlikely Santiago, a notoriously private guy, would bother alerting me to anything.

"There is one other thing to consider, though," she said.

"Which is?"

My lady paused for a moment, and her eyelashes fluttered, something she tended to do when taking time to think before she spoke. After a moment, she squared herself away and faced me directly.

As she did so, her leg brushed against mine, and for a micro second I lost track of the conversation we'd been having.

"Before you go off to do your savior thing," Talia said, "do you think Santiago really is dirty in some way?"

"Let's say the thought has crossed my mind about a hundred times in the last couple of years."

"And?" she asked.

"And I don't really know. There's no doubt he lives beyond his means."

"Are you sure? Do you even know what his means are?"

"Believe it or not, I looked it up once. I can't speak to Santiago especially, but the average police lieutenant in the state makes around a hundred grand a year."

Talia's eyes popped. "I wouldn't have guessed that much. That's more than some of our professors make."

"Yeah, but it's a lot less than some of them earn as well. After all, don't you deans have some sliding scale. You know, the fewer classes they teach the more take home they earn?"

She looked as if she wanted to throw a pillow at me.

"Stop and think about it, though," I said. "I've heard from a lot of the cops who come to work out at The Blaster. With recruiting problems the last several years, hell the entry level rookies are making north of fifty grand, and that's before they even set foot on the street."

"Does Santiago live a low six-figure life style?"

I shook my head. "Not even close. Hell, his slacks collection alone has to run over fifty grand."

She gave me a look. "Back to my original question then. Despite his motives, is it possible Councilman Farrell is right? Is Santiago crooked?"

I stared at her wall for a moment. It was a nice, pale blue wall. Should have been a calming color, but at the moment it wasn't doing anything for me.

"I don't really know," I said, "but I am sure of one thing. Farrell isn't going after Santiago because he thinks he's crooked. He's going after him because the lieutenant crossed him a couple of times while doing his duty."

"Wouldn't that be reason enough to help out?" Talia asked.

"Yeah," I said. "I guess it would be."

CHAPTER TWENTY-NINE

"No, Blondie, you cannot look at official police files, especially those involving minors."

"Boy," I said, "promote a guy up, even temporarily, and he forgets who his friends are."

Nichols scowled.

I did my best not to look terrified.

"What are you even doing here?" he asked. "Don't you have an actual client you should be working for?"

"Walk and chew gum, buddy. He's holed up in his new hotel room, and he promised me he wouldn't leave."

"And of course up to now he's been such a stalwart when it comes to doing what he should."

It was nine o'clock the next morning. I'd gone right from Talia's to the station and found Nichols, as I'd half expected, hunched behind Santiago's desk, doing his best to keep things running during the boss's enforced sabbatical.

"So with your boy all snugged away, you decided to pop in and brighten my day?"

"My, we are in a foul mood, aren't we?"

"Getting fouler by the minute, buddy. Tell me, just for the hell of it, why do you want to see what we've got on the Jackson High drug bust?"

"Because something doesn't make sense," I said.

"That could be the police force motto. We could get tee-shirts with it as a slogan 'Something doesn't make sense'. You care to elaborate a bit?"

"Sure." I slumped down in my chair and stretched my legs in front of me. "You act on a regular tip, and you round up a bunch of teenagers involved in dealing. What was it by the way?"

"Believe it or not, seriously high-end heroin. Hardly anything mixed in, almost hundred percent pure."

I frowned at him. "Hadn't even been stepped on?"

"If it was stepped, only with the lightest possible touch."

"Okay, you've busted a bunch of teenagers playing drug kingpin. Interesting, especially considering the pedigree of some of the parents, but except for the quality of the stuff it's not exactly earth-shaking."

"The quality of the stuff is what makes it rather noteworthy," Nichols said.

"Maybe, but you're still talking a high-school dope ring."

"So?"

"So why does Mark Farrell go ballistic in the city council and begin hounding the head of the detective squad? What does it get him?"

Nichols gave me a look like he was about to make me go sit in the corner. "Because one of those pedigreed kids you mention was his own. The golden boy Troy Farrell."

"Troy ever been in trouble with the law before?"

Nichols slitted his eyes. "Now we're getting close to stuff I can't tell you, Sam."

"Doesn't really matter if he has or hasn't. Either way, we're not exactly talking the caper of the century here. Farrell gets his kid a good lawyer, someone like Bernie Lyman, and it gets pled down to jaywalking."

"Probably," Nichols said. "That part's out of my hands."

"But the point is, Josh, why the big move on Santiago? Why pick a fight with the lieutenant over something relatively trivial? Does it have anything to do with the whole Marlowe thing?"

"I don't see how," Nichols said. "Mayor Windbag is counting down the days to the next election, which he's made it clear he's not taking part in."

"So why the big push on Santiago?"

"Maybe because Farrell's a complete douchebag."

"Or maybe there's more."

Nichols pushed himself away from the desk, got up, and went over to a coffeemaker perched on a tan filing cabinet. He glanced my way. I shook my head, and he proceeded to make himself a cup, no sugar but an awful lot of cream.

He made his way back to the desk, took a long swallow of the coffee, and placed the Styrofoam cup down. "The department has to walk carefully here."

"If you recall about a year ago," I said, "that seems to be a pattern with you guys when it comes to the city leaders. Have the Staties been called in yet?"

Because Providence is a relatively small city, with a proportionately small force, there really is no official Internal Affairs squad. Problems of that kind, especially concerning higher-level officers, are usually turnkeyed over to the State Highway Patrol for investigation.

"Not yet they haven't. Would be kind of awkward, seeing as there's no actual charges yet against the lieutenant."

"Then what the hell are they calling it?" I asked.

"At the moment it's a quote—informal inquiry—unquote."

"Spearheaded by Farrell," I said.

Nichols took another long drink.

"What all do you know about Mark Farrell?" he asked.

"Not all that much. Except he seems to own half the car dealerships in town."

Nichols nodded. "Farrell Nissan, Farrell Honda, and Farrell Toyota."

"Don't forget the BMW dealership," I said.

"How could I? His kid was driving a brand-new Z-4 when we made the move on him."

"So?" I asked.

"So say Farrell's a complete doofus, okay. Say he can't stand the thought of his kid being outed as a low-grade dealer, fair enough. And say he's had it in for the lieutenant ever since the Marlowe thing."

"I hate to tell you this, Josh. But you're making my point for me."

He finished off the coffee, crumpled up the cup, and made an easy two-pointer into the green metal trash basket in the corner.

"But none of that," he said, "explains why he's taking now to go after Santiago."

"Unless there's something more," I said.

Nichols nodded. "Unless there's something more."

"Looks like someone needs to look a little closer into the Farrell clan," I said.

"Cops can't do it. Not without unleashing thirty different kinds of hell on everyone."

"Then I guess someone else needs to," I said.

CHAPTER THIRTY

I LEFT THE STATION AND HEADED TOWARDS the Radisson. Coming out of the elevator on the third floor, I walked to the third door down and knocked.

Then, before he would have a chance to answer, I used the second of two keys he'd been given last night and let myself in.

Carson was sitting on the sofa, wearing a blue bathrobe, drinking coffee from a Styrofoam cup.

I nodded to him, but before either of us could say anything, my new phone buzzed. Pulling it out, I saw it was Nichols calling.

"I forgot to tell you when you were here," he said, "one thing you can say about the feds is they can speed things up when they really want to."

"Oh yeah?" I asked.

"Yeah. We fingerprinted the guy who survived your little roadside fracas yesterday along with the one you put down. Ordinarily, even with modern tech, it could take forever to run a search through all the systems out there."

"I always thought you didn't bother with much more than a statewide check," I said.

"And most of the time you'd be right. But considering where our original victim hailed from, it seemed pretty obvious to check all the databanks, including the federal ones."

"Uh huh."

"And say what you want about your new best friend Hendricks, but he made a call or two and expedited things for us."

"Okay."

"You're going to love this," Nichols said. "Both of those yahoos are from California."

"I pretty much figured that based on the suntans," I said.

"But did you figure they were both licensed security guards?"

"Come again?"

"Actually, let me rephrase," Nichols said. "They were formerly licensed as security guards. Within the last year or so, both of them, for separate reasons and working for difference companies, were fired and had their credentials yanked."

"For what?" I asked.

Nichols paused while I guessed he consulted some notes. "Gary Lockwood, that's the one you did your target practice on, was let go from Orion Security because of some missing jewelry in a store in the mall he was posted to."

"Hold on there, Josh. You saying the guy was a mall cop?"

"I am."

"God, I didn't even know mall cops were still a thing. Don't mention it to Carson or he'll get the idea to do a TV series about it."

"At the moment," Nichols reminded me, "Carson's your problem. Not mine."

"Oh, yeah. I forgot. What about the other guy?"

"Name Roy LaRue, believe it or not. He had a slightly cushier gig for Oversight, Inc. He was part of the permanent staff on site at some multi-gazillionaire's mansion."

"He get canned for stuff missing too?" I asked.

"Not exactly. More like getting a little up close and personal with the rich guy's daughter. It was right on the borderline of statutory rape, but they let it go because the guy lost his job and license."

"What have those guys been doing since then?" I asked.

"Far as anyone knows, they've been bouncing around the L.A. area not doing much of anything."

"Not doing much doesn't usually put food on the table," I said.

"True. But there's no records of any other criminal activity, either before or since."

"Their prints were in the system because they had to be bonded and licensed by their companies, right?"

"That's right."

"Anything on the three who tried to ambush us in his hotel room?"

"Not yet. The feds have pretty much taken that over, and Hendricks's cooperation is only going so far. Since his boys were on site for that, he's considering those three his sole domain."

"Okay, keep me posted," I said as I hung up.

Next, I made a call to the gym.

Keri Eckland answered. "Sure, Sam, everything's cool. Lisa's not in right now. You want me to have her call you?"

"Naw, just let her know I may be out a few more days than I'd expected. I'm sure you guys got it under control, but go ahead and call me if you need anything."

"We were talking yesterday. Lisa told me she's been practicing at signing your signature. We figured we'd close early this afternoon, go shopping, and cut the checks in your name. Got a problem with that?"

"Not as long as you don't have a problem staying within my overdraft limit," I said.

"Which is?" Keri asked.

"If I told you, you'd start looking for a new job," I said.

"Then maybe we'll stay here and work like usual," Keri said.

"Good idea."

After I hung up, I glanced over at Carson as he finished draining his cup of coffee. "What's first on the agenda today?" he asked.

"The very first thing is to run by my place so I can change clothes. After that, we're going to take the most immediate of your problems and tackle it first."

"Which is the most immediate?"

"The feds are the nice guys, though they may not act like it all the time. We need to take care of the other problem first."

Something jumped behind Carson's eyes. "You mean whoever it was who killed Wendy and these guys who came after you and me?" he asked.

I nodded. "And we've got two problems with them."

"Two?" His eyes jumped again.

I motioned to him to finish dressing and get ready to go. He had on navy blue slacks, socks and a teal-colored silk shirt, but nothing else. He went into his bedroom and, leaving the door open, began rooting through his suitcase. "What two?" he asked.

I walked over and looked out the window, craning my head as far as I could to each side.

"What two?" he repeated behind me.

I turned and saw he'd added dark blue loafers and an off-tan sport coat to his appearance.

"You ready?" I asked.

Carson nodded. "What two?"

"The feds, believe it or not, are the least of your worries," I said.

Carson went a little pale again, but at least this time he didn't tremble or shake. "Yeah?"

"Yeah," I said. "Before anything else, we have to figure out a way to get Wendy's clients off your back."

"And you have an idea how to do that?"

"I do," I said, "though it's kind of a long shot.

CHAPTER THIRTY-ONE

FIVE MINUTES LATER, WE WERE BACK in the Cherokee and heading out.

"You made some phone calls before we left," Carson said.

"Yep. Three of them in fact."

"To whom?"

I debated telling him. On the one hand, his life was on the line in whatever the heck was actually going down. On the other, it would probably take twice as long to explain to Carson as to a regular person, and at the moment I didn't feel like I had the patience.

After a couple of seconds consideration, the first won out. If Carson didn't deserve to know what was going on, at least as much of it as I knew, who did?

"The first call was to the man we're on our way to meet. The second was to my buddy on the cop force to get the number for Special Agent Hendricks."

"And the third was to Hendricks?" Carson asked.

I nodded. "You've got it."

"So who is this first guy we're meeting?" Carson asked.

"A couple of questions for you first," I said. "Troy LaRue and Gary Lockwood."

"Yeah?"

"Those names mean anything to you?"

He turned away from me and stared out the windshield for a

moment, his eyes narrowed. Then he shook his head. "Can't say as they do? Should they?"

"Names of the two guys who tried to gun me down yesterday afternoon. They're from your neck of the woods."

"California?"

"L.A. to be precise."

Carson gave me a lopsided grin. "Come on, man. You know how many people live in the Los Angeles basin? It's not like your little burg here."

"We all don't exactly know each other on a first name basis here," I said. "But since for some reason they decided to take a run at me, and you're from the same general area, it's an obvious question."

"Yeah, you're right. Sorry, man. I'm still kind of hyped up from those dudes jumping us last night. Cops have any line on them yet?"

As we came to a red light, I glanced over at him. I've seen my fair share of people come down from all sorts of violence, including gunfights, and Carson didn't seem all that hyped to me. At least, no more than what I took for his normal state. Maybe he had a little more toughness than I gave him credit for.

Or maybe he still thought he was slow-walking through a TV script and none of this was real.

Then again, it had been several hours and, assuming he'd had a decent night's sleep, maybe he'd had time to shake a lot of it off.

"If they've ID'd those others, I haven't heard yet," I said.

"What about the federal end?" Carson asked.

"What do you mean?"

"Don't you have some sort of contact in the government? You know, some righteous guy who's fed up with bucking the bureaucracy for years and is ready to do the right thing, no matter what it costs him?"

Looked like my second guess was the correct one.

"Carson," I said, "we're going to see a guy, and while we're around him I really need you to tone down the cops and robbers movie talk. We're in the real world now, not HBO."

He settled back in his seat and gave me silence. I didn't know if he was offended or confused and at the moment didn't really care. All I wanted was quiet for a few minutes.

"So who is this guy?" Carson asked about ninety seconds later.

I sighed. I wasn't sure exactly how much I wanted to tell him because I knew without a doubt he'd get the wrong idea.

Or maybe the right idea.

"He's a guy I know who's, associated, with some people who may be able to help us out."

In my peripheral vision I could see him tense up.

"What kind of people?"

"People," I said. "Nothing to worry about."

"He a criminal of some kind?"

I didn't want to answer directly but knew if I didn't Carson's imagination would run even wilder than usual.

"How about we say he's involved with some shady groups and leave it at that," I said.

"He's going to gun me down?" Carson asked.

"What? No, John. He's not."

"He's going to turn me over to them for a ransom, or some sort of favor?"

"Who's them?"

"You know. The people Wendy was working for. The drug cartels and such back home."

"No," I said with as much patience as I could pull up. "He's not going to do that either. At least, I don't think so."

"You don't think so!" What started out as a bark changed, mid-sentence, to a squeak. "What do you mean you don't think? Isn't this guy a friend of yours?"

"Friend would be exaggerating a little," I said. "More like a dude I've had a few interactions with."

"What happens if he decides to shoot me down to get in good with the boys back West?"

I shrugged, by this point not even bothering about changing his delusions. "Let's hope it doesn't get to that."

"But is this guy trustworthy?"

"Trustworthy's a little strong. Let's say I trust him to work in his own interest."

"And his interest in helping me out is what, exactly?"

"Give me time," I said. "I'm still working on that part of it."

I'd called Sean O'Flaherty the night before and had to work my way through two layers of his boys before speaking to the man himself. O'Flaherty had agreed almost immediately, which had me worrying we may be walking into something, despite the assured attitude I was showing Carson.

I pulled into the parking lot of the main, and only, mall in Providence and drove around to the part of the lot that fronted the Target store at one end. I turned off the ignition.

"A Target?" Carson asked. "We're meeting a major player in the underworld in a Target?"

"Don't worry about it," I said. "There's something else we have to talk about."

"Yeah? What's that?"

"When you guys flew out here, did Wendy have any extra luggage?"

"How would I know? Like I said, she hardly ever traveled with me."

"How many bags did she have?" I asked.

"I don't know. Six or seven, I guess. Why? What's that got to do with anything?"

I took a deep breath. "This guy we're meeting came into my gym the other day."

"Yeah?" Carson was looking sideways at me.

"He said the word going around is Wendy was carrying three million dollars in some form or other. You know anything about that?"

Carson twisted sideways in his seat to look at me full on. "Three million dollars?"

"That's what the man said."

"Damn, guy. You know how much space three million dollars takes up?"

"Depends on the denomination of the bills," I said. "And it didn't necessarily have to be in cash. Could have been some other form."

"Yeah, but, geesh Sam. I thought you said she was coming out here to turn herself in to the feds."

"That's what Hendricks says. Could be something else going on. Or maybe two things at once. I'm guessing you didn't know anything about the money?"

He thought about it a minute, giving that scrunched look that for Carson meant serious contemplation. "Sounds like insurance," he said.

"Insurance?"

"Yeah," Carson said. "Like she was planning on going under, you know getting away from it all, and she brought the dough along to make things a little more comfortable?"

I was shocked, almost losing my breath as Carson for once came up with a solid idea.

It was a consideration. The main problem I saw being that if Wendy was planning on entering the protection program, the feds would have tight control over what she did and didn't bring with her.

There was no way any halfway-competent administrator would let a potential witness walk around with three million dollars, in whatever form it took, free and clear.

Still, it made a kind of sense, remarkable seeing as how it came out of Carson's brain, but before I could consider it much more, a dark blue Toyota SUV with smoked windows pulled in to park two slots down from us.

"That's him," I said.

Carson craned his neck. "A Toyota? What kind of godfather shows up to a meet in a Toyota?"

"The kind who's doing his best not to be noticed," I said. "Don't let the Toyota fool you. This is a real bad guy we're meeting. A genuinely bad man."

"So why'd he offer to help us?"

"That's what we're about to find out," I said as the passenger door of the Toyota opened up and O'Flaherty stepped out.

He was wearing a light gray suit, black shirt opened up at the neck, and black kidskin loafers. A pair of black Oakleys covered his eyes as he looked both ways before crossing over to the Cherokee.

Far as I could tell, the Toyota only had the driver in it, but with those windows it was hard to tell. I did a quick glance around the parking lot, this early in the day not all that full. I couldn't spot any of O'Flaherty's boys anywhere around, which didn't mean they weren't there.

I was glad I'd dressed up a bit, at least by my standards. I was wearing a light blue silk sport coat over my blue tee-shirt to conceal the gun on my hip.

As complicated as things seemed to be getting, it didn't feel very wise to be walking around without a weapon.

O'Flaherty opened the driver's side rear door and climbed in. He settled into the seat behind me but didn't take off the Oakleys.

"Sam," he said. It was hard to tell where his eyes were looking but his head didn't even nudge towards Carson. "This the guy?"

I half turned in my seat to face O'Flaherty head on.

"It is," I said. "Thanks for coming."

After one good look at our visitor, Carson had turned to stare out the front windshield.

"He's bringing a bit of heat into our town," O'Flaherty said. "Two gun battles in twenty-four hours."

"Actually," I said, "it looks more like his business partner brought the heat. He was along for the ride."

"Yeah, but his girl partner is dead now, and he's the one has to carry the marker for the heat."

Carson finally turned to look at both of us. "Marker?"

"Be quiet, John," I said. "Sean, what would you say if I told you he didn't know anything about what his partner had been up to?"

"Comes right down to it, doesn't matter what I'd say. Word's already getting around, and it matters what the boys back west would say."

"Actually. . ." Carson began, but I cut him off.

"Come on, Sean. You're the man on the scene here. Sure it matters what you think."

O'Flaherty shook his head. "In that case, if you told me numb nuts here didn't know anything about the Truell woman's activities, or the money in question, I'd say either he's a real skillful liar or you're going soft in the head, Sam."

Carson opened his mouth, but with a slashing motion of my hand I kept him quiet. "Yeah," I said, "that's about what I figured you'd think. Take a good look at him, though, and tell me this. If you were laundering cash for some big-time players, would you take a guy like him into your confidence?"

Carson frowned but kept quiet.

Maybe he was getting the hang of how this worked.

"No one's saying they were thick as, ah, thieves," O'Flaherty said. "But there's no way they worked together as long as they could and he didn't have some ideas. Far as that goes, from what I understand she never accompanied him on business trips. Didn't he kind of wonder why now?"

Carson looked at me. I nodded.

"I did," he said, "but figured she just wanted to see the other side of the business."

Points to Carson for keeping quiet about the whole federal angle. Bringing it up now would only complicate things unnecessarily.

O'Flaherty made a noise that from someone less imposing and dangerous would have been a snort. "So what are we doing here, Sam?"

"What we're doing is trying to get a little breathing room for John here. Someone's already taken a run at both him and me a couple of times, and we'd like to figure out a way to get it stopped."

"I heard about that," O'Flaherty said. "But there's a bit of a problem there."

"Such as?" I asked

"Such as I only got the word second hand. You know, on the street."

Carson looked as blank as ever, but I did some quick, furious thinking.

"You telling me," I said, "that no one gave you a heads up they were coming into your territory?"

"Gets a little worse than that, Sam."

"Really? What could be worse than freelancers coming in unannounced?"

O'Flaherty's face was as neutral as I'd ever seen it, but even under his silk suit I could see his shoulders tense. "God's honest truth, Sam. Not only didn't I know ahead of time, I can't find out much about them."

Carson's expression had gone from blank to hopelessly confused. To him, the mobster and I were probably talking a different language.

"How's that possible?" I asked. "Even the coming in under cover is hard to believe. You saying you tried to track it down and couldn't?"

"Of course I tried to track it down. The last thing you want in any territory, even one as small as this, is outsiders showing up out of the blue. Once I heard, I spent most of last night pushing every button I can think of, but couldn't find out word one."

"Damn," I said, feeling a little pulse of hopelessness. I was just realizing I'd kind of assumed O'Flaherty and his connections could get me out of all this.

"You've got to understand," O'Flaherty continued. "Organized crime isn't nearly as organized as it used to be."

"Which means someone could have come into your territory for the hell of it and not let you or the guys above you know."

"It's possible, but it doesn't happen very often."

For an instant, out of the corner of my eye, I thought I saw a bit of a smirk appear on Carson's face. It vanished almost as soon as it appeared.

"So what do we do now?" I asked.

"That's easy," O'Flaherty said.

I could almost see Carson's heart leap in his chest.

"Yeah?" I asked.

The mobster grinned. "Some group or gang may be running their own thing, but if we have something they want, they'll come out of the woodwork and do business. How about you have your buddy here turn over the three million to me, and we'll use it as bait to get to the bottom of this."

"That's not too funny, Sean."

"No, it isn't. But neither is trying to play pattycake with really bad guys, whoever the hell they are. Hell, Sam, you and I have known each other for a while, and since there's no one else around but numb nuts here to testify, I've got no problem pointing out that in something like this I'm definitely the low guy on the totem pole."

I sucked in my breath. It was common knowledge O'Flaherty, and Paddy O'Brien before him, were merely the local faces for the Chicago and St. Louis outfits, or what was left of them in current times, but it was the sort of thing that was understood without being flat-out spoken.

Was it possible he was being deliberately kept out of the loop?

"Are you saying," I asked, "that you don't have enough juice to broker a deal?"

O'Flaherty frowned, and his eyes narrowed a bit. "I didn't say that, Sam. What I meant is there's several layers I have to run it by. Got me?"

I nodded and breathed a little easier. Even though I'm a big, tough guy, hell, almost a reality TV star, Sean O'Flaherty is not someone to cross unless you have both eyes wide open.

"Why would you do this?" Carson suddenly blurted out. "These are your people. Why would we think you'll help us over them?"

I kept my face straight while wanting to punch him in the mouth.

O'Flaherty twisted in his seat to give Carson his full gaze. The air inside the car almost crackled, and I wondered how fast I could get to the weapon in my console.

"You're not too bright, are you mister?" O'Flaherty asked.

Carson lurched back against the car door, his momentary burst of courage all used up. "I didn't . . ."

"You think you're some kind of rich slicker visiting in the small town? Let me straighten you out."

Afraid he was going to strike out at Carson, I tensed, though sitting as I was twisted in a car seat I didn't have a lot of maneuvering room.

"I'm sorry," Carson began, "I just . . ."

"Shut your mouth and let me explain a few things." O'Flaherty took a deep breath, then nodded at me. I relaxed again. "I personally don't give a damn about you or your problems. Sam here's another matter. For reasons that aren't germane at the moment, I care what he thinks. But I'd even throw that aside for another consideration. Ask me what it is."

Carson stayed silent, his mouth twisted into a grimace.

O'Flaherty leaned into him a little. Only a couple of inches, but enough to intrude into Carson's space. "I said ask me what it is."

Glancing down, I saw Carson's fingers digging into his pants legs.

"What is it?" he asked.

O'Flaherty leaned back in his seat, and somehow in the one motion I felt all the tense energy drain out of the Cherokee's interior. "My town," he said. "Providence here. I may only be middle management level, actually pretty much a gopher for the big boys a little farther east, but this is my town all the same. And I don't like the idea of running gun battles going on within its limits, especially when the participants don't clear it with me first. Make sense to you?"

Carson nodded without saying a word.

O'Flaherty turned a bit to look at me. "Clear enough?"

I nodded. "I'll wait to hear from you," I said, "but in the meantime, tell the boys not to get too itchy if they see us talking to the feds as well."

"Why would you be doing that?" O'Flaherty asked, his eyes narrowing again. To my side, Carson tensed up even more than before.

"Because while your amigos have lost their golden goose and think Carson here can help them out, the feds are probably thinking the same thing. They haven't let him out of their sight since yesterday. Meaning our next stop is to convince them he knows nothing, sees nothing, hears nothing."

O'Flaherty shook his head. "I'm starting to think it would be a whole lot easier to pull out my piece and do both of you right now."

In the passenger seat, Carson began shaking. Another minute of this, and I'd probably have to have the seats steam cleaned.

"Knock it off, Sean. You know you've got no reason to shoot us, especially with so many people wandering around this parking lot."

O'Flaherty chuckled. "'Course not. I just wanted to see how your boy here would react when I suggested it."

"At least he's not huddled down on the floorboards."

"Good point." O'Flaherty opened his door and stuck a leg out. "I'll see what I can do, but if I were you, I'd keep any contact with the federal boys and girls on the down low."

"No point making your tribe any more jittery than they already are?" I said.

O'Flaherty grinned. "That's about the idea."

"Okay," I said, "now I've got one more thing."

"Oh?"

"Yeah." I turned to Carson. "John, would you step outside of the car for a moment."

"Huh?" Carson asked.

"Step outside please. I need to talk to Sean here in private."

CHAPTER THIRTY-TWO

"SOMETHING ELSE ON YOUR MIND?" O'FLAHERTY asked after Carson had exited the Cherokee. He stood leaning against the front fender well as I rolled the windows up.

"Yeah," I said. "Something unrelated to all this."

"Okay."

"Did you hear about the cops rounding up a lot of high-schoolers looking to deal heroin last month?"

"You mean those preps from Jackson High?"

"I don't think they're called preps any more, Sean. But yeah, that's who I mean."

"Remember hearing about it," O'Flaherty said. "So what?"

"Know anything about it that wasn't made public?" I asked.

"You asking if I or any of the boys were mixed up in that?"

"Asking if you know anything about it."

O'Flaherty chuckled. "Could I assume you're asking on behalf of a certain police lieutenant?"

The fact he knew about that didn't surprise me. Not a lot went on in the middle section of the state he wasn't on top of.

"Assume away," I said, "because some people are kind of wondering what's going on."

"Santiago's a tough guy, according to what the boys in Chicago tell me. He'll come out of it okay."

"That's my question," I said. "What does he have to get out of?"

"The way I hear it, some of the city leaders are coming for his job."

"That's about it, yeah," I said. "Can you tell me anything about it? Even on background?"

"What's in it for me?"

"A sense of pride in fulfilling your civic duty?" I suggested.

Now his chuckle became a full-out laugh. "Doubtful. But what the hell, I've got some time to kill. Ask your questions."

Outside the car, Carson was beginning to prance. I figured I'd better wrap things up quick or he was likely to go skipping down the parking lot.

"The way I hear it," I said, "what those kids were trying to unload wasn't some low-grade stuff that had been stepped on half a hundred times."

"Meaning it was almost pure," O'Flaherty said.

"Yeah. I'll ask it straight out, Sean, you or your boys have anything to do with it?"

O'Flaherty shook his head. "Despite the purity of the product, we tend not to do business with amateurs. But if you want to help your cop buddy, you're looking in the wrong direction."

"Meaning?" I asked.

"Meaning knowing the original source of their product isn't important."

"Okay," I said, drawling out the word several syllables in an attempt to allow my mind to keep up.

"You know the old saying," O'Flaherty asked, "about apples not falling far from trees?"

"Yeah."

He opened the rear door and stepped out. As he did so, Carson moved off the fender well and started to open his door, but I held up a hand to stop him.

"What about it?" I asked.

"Don't waste your time with the apple, go for the tree."

Obviously assuming he'd given me everything I needed, the mobster strolled over and got in the Toyota, which promptly drove away.

CHAPTER THIRTY-THREE

TURNED OUT DEALING WITH O'FLAHERTY AND the mob was a little bit easier, at least at first, than dealing with the feds. Leaving the mall, I turned right onto Main and pulled out my phone.

"You okay?" I asked Carson.

He nodded. If we were lucky, he was finally beginning to see the difference between the real world and entertainment

We made it about six blocks down Main Street before Carson said anything.

"I'm wondering how you happen to be friendly with a guy like that," he said. "From the way you described him, I'm assuming he's a killer."

We pulled up to a stoplight, and I glanced sideways at Carson. His face was pale, and he was learning forward a little towards me. The light turned green.

"Sure, he's a killer. When he feels he needs to. But most of the time he's more like he described himself: middle-management."

Carson considered a moment as I kept driving. This time of day, especially with the students in town, Providence traffic actually verges on stop and go.

"But how do you know him?" Carson asked as I got to another red light. We were close to our destination.

"I had a case a few years back that involved a relative of his," I said. "We crossed paths and ended up having to work together."

Carson continued mulling as I pulled into the parking lot of a chain coffee shop. I shifted into Park.

"I need you to go inside and get something to eat or drink, or both if you want. You've got to stay occupied for a while, maybe a quarter hour or more, then I'll come get you."

Carson glanced at the front of the shop. Three or four wrought iron tables and matching sets of chairs sat out front.

"Okay if I sit outside?" he asked.

I thought about it for a second.

"Probably better that way," I said.

"Better?"

"Sure. On the one hand, if anyone we don't like happens to swing by, you'll be spotted, but with this many people around you, plus everyone going through the intersection, anyone with half a brain wouldn't dare make a move."

Carson nodded. "I don't really want anything, though. I'll just take a seat here and wait for you to get back."

"Okay."

He gave me a look, and I realized my tone had been a little shorter than it probably should have been. I pointed across the street at an angle. "That's Logan Park. I'm meeting an F.B.I guy there in a couple of minutes. We're supposed to meet alone, but with the feds you never know. Plus, there may still be people on the other side trying to track you down. Stay out here, where anyone passing by can see you. That should cut down on the chance of anyone trying to pull anything."

Carson nodded, grasped the door handle, and opened the door. He stopped halfway out. "You're not going to jam me up in any way, are you?"

The words sounded like the same sort of blather I'd been hearing a lot from him the last few days. The tone, however, was a little more serious and down to earth.

"I'm doing my best to get you out of this mess, John. That's all."

"To earn your daily rate," he said.

I nodded. "That's right. Now go get something to drink, and let me try to fix this."

Carson blinked a couple of times, then got out of the car. "I appreciate it, Sam," he said before shutting the door and taking a seat at a nearby table.

I put the Cherokee into Drive and headed towards the park, wondering if I could possibly be as confident as I'd sounded.

CHAPTER THIRTY-FOUR

I WAS KIND OF SURPRISED, WHEN I'D called him earlier, that Hendricks had agreed to meet me away from the police station. Since Providence is too small for an actual federal building, the night before he'd argued for and finally managed to snag a small office somewhere in the police station.

Since he'd impressed me the day before as a rather pain-in-the-ass type of bureaucrat, I took it as a possibly good sign both that he'd agreed to meet me in Logan Park and had allowed me to run around loose for several hours with John Carson, who Hendricks would have been justified taking into custody, even if he wouldn't have been able to make anything stick.

Logan is one of the nice little areas that make Providence something more than an ordinary town. Going back all the way to the early 19th Century, it has a decent-sized lake smack dab in the middle, along with walking paths, a playground, fountains, and of course, places to grill or BBQ.

It's fairly common in any type of weather to see people occupying the park, usually making their way along the walking trails, at almost any time of the day. But even with its popularity, there are enough dips, turns, and twists in the park to provide some degree of relative privacy without being completely cut off from the rest of the world.

As you go in from the south side, it doesn't take long to come upon a big green sign serving as a map to the area, and it was there I found Special Agent Hendricks waiting for me.

Besides the fed's phone number, Nichols had given me a little information about him so I'd have a better idea what I'd be dealing with. Among other things, he'd mentioned Hendricks was a former Army Ranger. As such, I'd have expected him to know a little about camouflage. But even in a park in the middle of the day, the fed wore a tan suit and solid blue tie with his suitcoat buttoned. He also had the standard Ray-Bans the Secret Service wore for decades, until it became too much of a cliché, and other government types had begun affecting over the years.

I walked up to him and nodded but didn't hold out my hand to shake.

Hendricks took a moment to lower his sunglasses and look around our section of the park.

No one here but us chickens.

"You made off with a material witness last night, mister," Hendricks said.

"Nobody ordered him to stay around," I said. "And he didn't feel like hanging around just then. Why didn't you swing by his hotel room and pick him up?"

"We did, only to find that he'd checked out. We hustled over to your place, but you didn't show up until this morning. And tracking down your phone didn't help us at all."

I raised up my hands in a kind of "aw shucks" gesture. "What can I say?"

"For starters, you can say where your boy is," he asked.

"Nearby," I said. "Figured it wouldn't hurt for you and me to talk first."

The fed slipped the glasses back on and thrust his hands into his pockets. "What's to talk about? It's a simple deal. He comes in, spills everything he knows about his late partner and their business, we take care of him after that."

"New identity, new home, new occupation?" I asked.

"Provided it comes to that, sure. If he wants to go that far and has something to give us. Either way, he's probably going to need our protection."

"Keep Wendy's former customers off his back for the rest of his life?"

"As much as we can," Hendricks said. "As soon as we know who they are."

"What a bargain."

The fed took his sunglasses off again, folded them, and put them in the breast pocket of his jacket. Unlike a lot of guys, without the glasses he actually looked tougher. Maybe something in the eyes told you he was deadly serious.

"It's the best bargain he's going to get. He needs to come in."

I nodded. "And what if he doesn't want to turn himself in? After all, he says he knows nothing about Wendy's sideline. And besides that, he's not entirely out from under a possible murder rap."

"I'd say that part's up to you to figure out," Hendricks said.

"Let's say the Truell killing falls somewhere else, maybe he still doesn't want to come in."

"Why wouldn't he? You think whatever West Coast outfits his partner was laundering for are going to care if he gets cleared of her murder? Either way, they're going to see him as a liability. You ever heard the term scorched earth?"

"But what if he's as ignorant as they come?"

"Excuse me?"

"On the level, Hendricks, Carson didn't know anything about what Wendy was doing. And he for damned sure didn't know she was about to throw her clients over and come in with you guys."

Hendricks glanced to both sides. "We're kind of sticking out here, Quinton. Let's walk or something."

I turned to the right, and the fed fell into step alongside me.

"What makes you think he's all that innocent?" Hendricks asked after a moment.

"Easy," I said. "Spend five minutes with the guy and you'll realize he's the last person you'd ever want to tell your secrets to."

"Predicated on her taking him into her confidence."

I had to think for a moment to translate the fed speak. "Yeah," I said. "Predicated on that."

"Doesn't mean he didn't find out some other way, on his own."

I gave that one about five yards worth of thought before shaking my head. "Maybe, but believe me. This guy only lives and breathes for television. Nothing else gets into his head. Except maybe movies."

"If he doesn't come in with us, sooner or later somebody's bullet's going to get into his head. Just on general principles. You know the kind of people the Truell woman was dealing with can't leave possible loose ends lying around."

"He knows that," I said, "and with a little persuasion I can get him willing to talk to you. But he doesn't want to do it as a convicted felon."

About then we came onto a curve, around which appeared two middle-aged women walking a pair of golden retrievers. Hendricks waited until the two had gotten out of earshot.

"You spoken to your buddies on the force lately?" he asked.

"Not for a few hours. Why?"

"Last I heard, they're getting nowhere on the Truell killing."

"They will," I said. "These are good cops in this town."

Hendricks paused and turned my way. "Never said they weren't. But maybe they had it right in the beginning."

"Meaning my client," I said.

Hendricks shook his head. "You know, I looked into you a bit. And I don't quite get it."

"How so?"

"From everything I heard, seems like you're not half bad as an investigator."

"Pretty strong compliment from a guy who wears Ray-Bans," I said.

"Whatever," Hendricks grunted. "The thing is, and this is going to sound like a dig but it isn't, you're kind of blue collar."

"You saying I should wear a suit like yours?"

"What I'm saying is everything I've heard about John Carson is he goes in for the flash and the glam. And that ain't you, no offense. So how'd he come to snag you on his side?"

I gave Hendricks the condensed version and wrapped it up as we reached about the halfway mark in our circuit of the park. The park's over a hundred acres in circumference, and he was taking it in stride.

Must have kept up with his Ranger training.

"This show" he said when I was done, "were you seriously considering it?"

"Don't really know. At first, it was a distracting lark for a day or so, but now it all seems to have blown up all over the place."

"And you really think the guy's legit? From what you describe, no one could be that big of a goof."

"True me, Hendricks. He is."

"Goof or not, doesn't mean he isn't a killer. Or worse."

"Test it out yourself. Talk with the guy, and you'll see what I mean."

We were alongside the lake now and, unusual for this time of day, hardly anyone was out and about. Kind of contradictory there. When I'd chosen the park, I knew it wouldn't be super crowded on a Friday, but seeing as it was close to noon, I'd figured there'd be enough around we could somewhat blend in.

'Course, I hadn't exactly counted on Hendricks wearing his Sunday Best clothing.

In unison, without either of us suggesting it, we stopped, turned, and looked at the small lake.

"He needs to come in," Hendricks said. "At the very least, we need to assure ourselves that he's as clean as you say."

It occurred to me Hendricks hadn't said anything about a stray three million dollars. Either he was cagier than he looked, or the government had somehow missed that particular angle.

At the moment, I didn't feel it my responsibility to clue them in.

"You're talking a debrief," I said.

"I am."

"Probably a pretty darned rigorous and intense one as well."

Hendricks looked at me. "For something like this, yeah. The L.A. office thought they had a major score on their hands, then the main player on the board gets out to this little college town and the whole thing falls apart."

"Their problem," I said, "not yours."

"All on the same team, buddy. Your boy may be as pure and white as you claim, but he still needs to come in and go through the ringer."

"He'll have to have a lawyer with him," I said, thinking that no matter how well-trained Hendricks and his people may be, they hadn't seen anything till they took on Bernie Lyman.

"I'll have to clear it with L.A., it's technically their case, but I don't see a problem with that. Only problem I see is on your end."

"How's that?" I asked.

"You think you're good enough to keep him alive long enough to come in to us?"

I didn't want Hendricks to know, but I'd been doing my best not to think about that. "Going to do my best," I said. "So far I'm one-oh."

We parted then, and a few minutes later I climbed into the Cherokee and drove out of the park. I hit the lights just right, and it took all of twenty seconds to get from the park over to the coffee shop.

I pulled into a conveniently open space right in front of the wrought iron tables where Carson had said he'd be and sat there wondering what to do next.

Mainly, I was wondering because the situation had suddenly gotten a lot more complicated.

John Carson was nowhere to be seen.

CHAPTER THIRTY- FIVE

I SUPPOSE HE COULD HAVE DECIDED TO step inside for a minute, maybe to use the bathroom. or get a second cup of coffee, but even as I the thought came to mind, I knew better.

Everywhere around the store, things looked normal. No upset people, no one screaming for help, not even a stray napkin fluttering around.

Peering closer at the table, I noticed a rectangular object that looked like an old-fashioned flip phone. Not knowing what else to do, I got out of the Cherokee and walked over to the table.

As I got there, a young man and woman, both about twenty-one and dressed in jeans and tee-shirts, came out of the shop. Both had drinks in their right hands and phones in their left. They automatically turned in the direction of the table I stood over.

I glared, and for a moment the guy, around five eleven and looking like he'd played some ball in his time, tensed up his shoulders and scowled at me. I glared even harder, and though he kept scowling his girl bumped him with her shoulder and nodded at another empty table a few feet away.

After another long moment, the he-man nodded to her and they walked off, leaving me free to sit down and stare at the phone on the table.

It was indeed an old-style flip model, the kind you can still buy at dollar stores in plastic packaging, sometimes known as burner phones.

Carson hadn't appeared yet, leading me to think he either wouldn't or couldn't show up.

I stared at the phone for about ten more seconds before it buzzed.

I flipped it open, feeling like Captain Kirk from *Star Trek.* "Yeah?"

"We've got your boy."

The voice was flat, almost unmodulated. It was empty enough of any sort of emotion I wondered if it was computer generated.

I took a deep breath and sat down at the table.

"Okay," I said, "what's the plan?"

"Your boy here knows the whereabouts of several million dollars." As we continued talking, the voice began to sound more and more like a really bored human.

"I'm not entirely sure he does know," I said. "But if he does, again so what?"

"We want the money, that's so what. And if we don't get it, it's going to be bad news for your boy here."

The repetition of the phrase "your boy" struck me as kind of odd. It almost sounded rehearsed.

I took a deep breath and looked around, wondering if whoever I was speaking with was somewhere within visual range.

Nothing out of the ordinary. Cars whizzing by, a few people walking their dogs in the park across the street, and the usual contingent of Providence citizens sitting around enjoying cups of way-too-expensive caffeinated concoctions.

Nobody lurking behind the nearby bushes, no one wearing an overcoat and Panama hat while twirling their mustache.

"Hey, man." The flat voice finally had a little emotion, maybe a hint of desperation. "You still there?"

"I'm here," I said. "But I'm not sure what you want of me."

"We want the money, dude. We get the money, and your guy here goes free. We don't get it and, well, you know."

"I don't know where the money is," I said, "or what form it's in. And I'm pretty sure Carson doesn't either. Why don't you put him on?"

"No way, dude. We know you can get to it. You grab the cash and wait for us to call you back."

I was beginning to get an odd feeling about this caller. I wasn't sure what, but something about him didn't feel legit.

For one thing, who the hell says "dude" anymore?

"I don't think it's in the form of cash," I said. "That would be way too bulky, and the cops would have found it in her room. Unless the killers took it."

There was a pause, a fairly long one, on the other end of the phone. I wasn't sure, it's harder to tell with cell phones than old-fashioned land lines, but I got the sense the person on the other end had covered the phone with their hand.

I waited, patiently. The young man who I'd scared off to another table still kept throwing me scowls from time to time.

A macho throwdown was the least of my worries right then.

Finally, Mr. Flat Voice came back on. "So she didn't have it in cash?"

"Probably not," I said. "More likely it's in some more disposable form."

"Like what?"

I thought of saying "bitcoin" just for the hell of it, but if the person on the other end knew anything at all about that, my bluff would be called.

"I don't know," I said. "All I know is it wasn't in cash and probably wasn't in her hotel room in any obvious form. Otherwise, the cops would have glommed on to it."

"Which means they don't have it?"

Damn, I realized too late I'd talked my way into a trap. "Not as far as I know."

"Then I guess, Mr. Detective, you had better get to detecting and find it, or else things won't look good for Mr. Producer here."

"How long do I have?" I said.

"Huh?" A puzzled note, as if he hadn't expected that question.

"To get the money. How long do I have to find it?"

"Just get it," the man said. "We'll call you back."

The longer the conversation went on, some of the flatness eased out of his voice, replaced by a rather high pitch.

"I assume you want me to keep this phone," I said.

"Uh, right. Keep it."

Something definitely off key here. "I could give you my number. That would make things easier."

"No, I mean, naw man. You keep that one, and we'll call you when it's time to make the tradeoff."

"Wait a minute," I cut in. "Is Carson okay?"

"We'll call you soon, man. Keep in touch." the voice said right before I heard a click from the other end.

Man?

CHAPTER THIRTY-SIX

"**W**HAT DO YOU MEAN YOU LOST him?" Hendricks voice grated in my ear.

I was still sitting at the table outside the coffee shop. The cheap phone that I'd found lying there was still resting on the table while I used mine to dial the fed.

"Just what I said."

"I left you barely five minutes ago. How do you know your client's in the wind?"

"Well . . ." I began before Hendricks cut me off.

"Crap! You had him waiting practically on site didn't you? Where was he?"

"You still in the park?" I asked.

"As a matter of fact, yes. I figured as irregular as all this was it would be best to get it recorded down while it was still fresh. I'm sitting in my car at this moment. Why?"

"If you pull out the west side and come straight south, you'll pick me up in no time at all."

There was a moment of silence. I imagined Hendricks was working on his scowl, trying to get it just right before speaking again. "You're at that friggin' coffee shop, aren't you?"

"Sitting right outside, Agent. Come on and join me. Looks like we've got more to talk about."

"I'm on my way. Two minutes tops. Don't you feakin' move, Quinton."

The fed was true to his word by about thirty seconds. I'd barely hung up before a black Ford SUV came screeching in, causing the seated patrons, including the guy who'd tried to stare me down and his girlfriend, to look up.

Hendricks practically slammed the SUV's door shut as he got out and stomped over to my table.

"Have a seat," I said, "want anything?"

"Cut the crap, Quinton." Yep, he had the scowl down to perfection, though he was bright enough to keep his voice low.

"If you don't sit down," I said, "everyone's going to continue to stare at us. If you sit down and pretend to act halfway normal, in a second they'll turn away and go about their business."

His shoulders tensed, and his hands clenched into half fists, before he visibly shook himself into some semblance of control.

He sat down across from me. "This is the goddamndest operation I've ever seen," he muttered.

A waitress came out the front of the shop and looked our way. I waved her off.

"Look," I said, "I don't blame you for being pissed. I'm not all too happy myself. But let's make sure we're both mad at the right thing." I used the edge of my hand to nudge the burner phone, still sitting on the table, over to him.

Hendricks may have been a blowhard, but he definitely wasn't a fool. He looked down at the phone but didn't pick it up. "What's this?"

I told him about the call. He dipped his head down to look closer at the phone, angling his head a couple of different ways. "Looks fairly standard. You say you picked it up when it rang?"

"Yeah, kind of a dumb move in hindsight. I took the call without thinking."

I expected a new outburst, but the fed surprised me by cracking a grin my way. "Don't kill yourself over it, it's instinct. No matter what's going on, a phone rings, chimes, or buzzes and we pick it up."

Reaching into his breast pocket, Hendricks brought out a pair of latex gloves, a pen, and a small plasticine bag with a blank label pasted on it.

"You a Boy Scout?" I asked. "Always come prepared?"

"When I'm on a case, yes." He wrote something on the bag's label, then pulled the gloves on and scooped the phone into the bag. "If these guys are pros, it'll be a dead end and won't tell us anything."

"And if they're amateurs?" I asked.

"We'll probably learn the lot number and that it was purchased at a dollar store somewhere, and it'll still be a dead end."

"So why bother with the evidence routine?"

"Like you said, it's routine. Besides, never can tell when you'll get lucky."

I found my feelings towards Hendricks starting to shift. At first, he'd come off as a typical narrow-minded government type, but he was starting to show a bit more than that.

"You're forgetting something," I said.

"Which is?"

"I'm supposed to wait for a call on that phone. What happens if it rings and I'm not around to answer?"

"When I get it to the lab, we won't leave it alone for a second. Somebody will answer it, and we can go from there."

"Correct me if I'm wrong, but isn't the nearest F.B.I. lab in St. Louis?"

"It is. Which is why I'm only taking it as far as the Providence PD to get it fingerprinted before I get it back to you. We can always track down the forensic info on it later."

"Like you say, I picked it up though."

"True. Which means the possibility of prints is probably zilch."

"But it's routine to check them out," I said.

Hendricks raised his right hand up in a gun motion and cocked his trigger finger at me. "I'll call you as soon as we've got it printed. Personally, though, I wouldn't hold my breath on them calling back."

"Because?" I asked.

"Because why do you think?"

I nodded, pretty sure we were both thinking in the same direction. "Because it feels a little too cliched. A little too like misdirection."

"And?"

"And if I knew where the money was, it could only be because Carson had told me."

Hendricks nodded. "In which case, why would they need you for anything when they have the man himself?"

I drummed my fingers on the table for a moment. "Something's wrong here," I said.

"Only one thing?"

I nodded. "Good point. There've been two runs at either me or Carson by gunmen."

"And of the ones we've managed to trace, no connection with the kind of people the Truell woman was supposedly working for," Hendricks said.

"And both of those, including the last one made in Carson's hotel room, the hoods seemed intent on killing him."

"Right."

"But this morning he's kidnapped instead," I said.

"Curiouser and curiouser."

"It gets even worse," I said. "Don't ask me details, but I spent part of the morning talking with a guy I know."

"A guy."

I nodded. "One who would know if there were any extra criminal types floating into town."

"Let me guess. This guy of yours is as much in the dark as the two of us are."

"Yep."

"Leaves us with two questions," Hendricks said.

I frowned, mainly to mix things up. "One, who killed Wendy Truell and is trying to kill John Carson."

"Two," Hendricks put in, "who went about this elaborate kidnapping. And Two-B, how'd they get away with it in broad daylight in only a few minutes?"

"If you think about it, all these questions can collapse into one general catch-all question."

Now it was Hendricks turn to nod. "Yeah. What the hell is going on here?"

CHAPTER THIRTY-SEVEN

I LEFT HENDRICKS AND HEADED OUT. AT the moment, I couldn't think of anything to do, and with both the feds and local cops on the case, plus Hendricks in possession of the burner phone, they didn't need any added manpower from me.

I decided to follow up on Sean O'Flaherty's comment the day before about apples and trees.

I went home, made a quick sandwich of smoked sausage, cheese, and BBQ sauce, then sat down at my computer, phone at hand. I looked up several pages online, called a couple of people I know in the banking business, and searched through some old newspaper stories that showed up online. It took a couple of hours, but by the time I finished, I thought I had a pretty clear idea of my next move.

I grabbed the silk jacket I'd been wearing earlier and shucked it on. The early afternoon had brought on temps in the high 70's, and I'd definitely have been more comfortable without the sport jacket. But I only had the haziest idea of what I was walking into and that, combined with the two gun battles the day before, left me not wanting to walk around unarmed.

Leaving my apartment, I hopped onto the Interstate and headed east. In less than five minutes I'd passed the city limits, and less than two minutes later was pulling into the huge parking lot, right off of a turnaround, of Farrell Toyota.

Of the handful of car dealerships the Farrell family owned, the Toyota was the longest-lasting, having been started by Roger

Farrell, grandfather of the current owner, nearly fifty years ago. Also, a couple of people I'd spoken with told me that, despite the fact Farrell dealerships were all over the area, the Toyota store was the location of Farrell's main office.

As I climbed out of the Cherokee, a young man, looking barely out of high school and wearing navy blue slacks, white dress shirt, and solid red tie came over to me.

With a smile, I waved him off and headed into the store. Once inside, it only took a moment to spot the main service counter, over against the west wall. Three young women, each wearing navy blue blazers and white blouses, worked behind the counter. Two of them were on the phone, and the third was tapping away at a keyboard.

I walked up to the one on her computer.

"Yes sir?" she said, looking up at me.

I gave her another smile, hopefully a friendlier one than I had to the kid outside, and asked to speak to Mark Farrell.

She frowned, a notch forming between her dark brown eyes. "Do you have an appointment?"

"Do I need one?" I asked, beaming my smile even wider.

There had been a time in my life when attractive young women reacted to that smile a certain way. More and more, however, when I tried it I usually got a look of granddaughterly affection.

Still, you take what you can get.

"I'm afraid so," the young woman said. "Mr. Farrell doesn't usually see anyone without an appointment."

She cast a quick glance up and down, and despite my silk sport coat I wondered if my jeans and tee shirt probably put me way down in the pecking order.

"If you'd like to . . ." she began as I leaned in a bit. Not far enough to be threatening, but enough to shrink her field of vision a bit.

"Tell him it's about Troy," I said.

She blinked. The counter person to her left hung up the phone and glanced over our way.

"I'm sorry?"

"Tell him it's about Troy," I repeated. "Trust me, you won't get in any trouble."

With her right hand, she reached to a phone beside her but didn't pick it up, only resting her hand on the set. "Can I tell him who's calling?"

I gave her another bright smile, a reward for cooperating, and pulled out the photostat of my license.

I held the license in front of her. She looked at it, looked up at me, then lowered her gaze to read it again.

"Let me see what I can do," she said as she lifted up the phone's handset.

I took a couple of steps back and half turned away to give her a little privacy to talk.

A minute later, out of the corner of my eye I saw her place the phone down.

"Mr. Farrell will be out in a minute."

I nodded my thanks and walked off a ways to look over a red Supra sitting in the showroom. Barely a minute later, I heard a man clear his throat behind me.

"Can I help you?"

I turned and gave him another of my beaming smiles, though not quite the wattage I'd used on his employee. "Good afternoon," I said.

I didn't reach out to shake hands, and neither did he.

"What can I do for you Mr. . . . . Quinton is it?"

"It is," I said. I looked around at the roughly thirty people, split between potential customers, sales reps, and sundry other employees, moving throughout my field of vision. "But I really think we should talk somewhere a bit more private."

The man in front of me frowned, though briefly. "You told Anne this was about Troy?"

I nodded. "That's right. Is that enough of a hint to get us some privacy?"

He stared at me for a moment, his face blank, then held out his left arm in an ushering motion.

"It is," he said, "Why don't you come with me?"

We walked into the bowels of the building and into the man's private domain.

CHAPTER THIRTY-EIGHT

M ARK FARRELL DIDN'T LOOK AT ALL like a car salesman. He was average height, right around five eight, and clearly did something to keep himself lean and trim. The tan two-piece suit he wore hung just right on his frame. He had about the darkest hair I'd ever seen in my life. So black I wondered if it came out of a bottle.

He was clean-shaven, in the middle of the afternoon looking as if he had shaved not five minutes ago. As he sat down at his desk and waved me to a set of three black webbed chairs arranged in front of the desk, his manicured nails glinted from the overhead lights.

"So what can I do for you, Mr. Quinton?"

Without saying anything, I took my license photostat from my pocket and handed it over to him.

He barely glanced at it.

"Yes, Anne out front informed me of your occupation. If it's work you're looking for, we already have a firm that handles any repossessions we need done."

"I already have a client," I said.

Farrell arched an eyebrow. "Oh?"

"The parents of one of the kids arrested with your son," I said with a perfectly straight face

Farrell pursed his lips and sat back in his chair. "Which one?"

I shook my head. "Sorry, can't say. Confidentiality and all that."

Which would go a long way towards helping me get away with this little stunt.

"It probably won't be all that tough for me to find out," he said. "After all, I'm familiar with most of the families involved."

I spread my hands. "So go ahead and find out. I can't tell you myself."

Farrell leaned forward again, steepling his fingers and resting his chin on them. "In that case, Mr. Quinton, what exactly can I do for you?"

"It's like this, Mr. Farrell. Obviously, my clients didn't hire me to prove their kid innocent. After all, the bunch of them were caught pretty much red-handed."

"Which may or may not mean anything, but go on."

"So what they asked me to do was come up with anything, no matter how slight, that could possibly mitigate their son's sentence."

"Mitigate," Farrell said.

"Uh huh. And as I thought it over, there was one aspect of the whole thing that kept coming back to me."

Farrell pulled his sleeve back to look at his watch. "Mr. Quinton, could we speed this up? I don't know about you, but it's rather late in the afternoon and I still have a lot of . . ."

"The purity," I said.

That stopped him in his tracks. The car dealer narrowed his eyes. "Come again?"

"According to the police report, the material confiscated in the bust was damned near pure, as if it had come right off the boat."

Farrell grinned. "You mean over the border, don't you?"

"No, sir. Most drugs that come from down south come through our ports, not across the line, but I'm sure as a regular citizen you wouldn't know that."

Farrell's jaw hardened a little. "Okay."

"Well you see, Mr. Farrell. I don't know how much you know about dope, but having material that hasn't been stepped on at least half a dozen times by the time it gets this far into the country is pretty unheard of."

Farrell tried to look cool, but I saw his hands kind of tightening

up. "If you have a point, I really wish you'd get to it. I have a lot of
. . ."

"The point is it would be almost impossible for a bunch of high-schoolers, even ones as well off as your son and his friends, to come across junk of such high quality by themselves. The cops feel, and I kind of agree with them, that they must have filched the stuff from someone else."

"Filched," Farrell said.

I shrugged. "Okay, stole."

"And exactly how do you know what the police are think-ing? For that matter, how do you happen to know what's in their reports?"

Now it was my turn to lean back and look cool and collected. "I've been operating in this town for quite a few years, Mr. Farrell. I've got my share of contacts here and there."

I wasn't sure, but I thought I saw a faint line of sweat appear on the guy's forehead. "Are you somehow tied in with that damned lieutenant?" he asked.

I laughed. "Santiago? He's just a dumb cluck. Doesn't even know what the guys under him are doing. If you ask me, you're doing the town a service by trying to get him axed."

"I didn't ask you, and what goes on in city council meetings . . ."

"Isn't the business of the citizens?" I asked.

He stopped again, and now I could for sure see the guy sweating.

I pulled my little spiral notebook out of my jeans and flipped it open. "Since I was wondering where the kids got their stuff from, I figured the obvious thing to do was look close to home. After all, even with the way young people are plugged in these days, it's not all that easy to walk down the street and stumble upon high-grade heroin. At least not in quantities big enough to sell and make a profit."

Farrell said nothing, but his glare said plenty.

"I began digging into all the families involved, all except my clients of course. And like I said, I've been in this city a long time and know a lot of peepholes to look through."

I paused for a minute and glanced down at the notebook in my hand. I flipped over a couple of pages, really milking it for all it was worth.

Farrell stayed silent. If I listened really hard I could probably hear his heart thudding.

"And of course," I looked back up at him, "since you're the one trying to make it especially difficult for the cops, I took an extra hard look at you."

"I don't follow."

"Well see, most of the parents involved, even in those cases where they're divorced from each other and don't get along all that well, are taking basically the same course. Hire the best lawyer or lawyers they can, paint themselves as beleaguered parents doing the best they can and see what rolls. Only one set of parents, or rather one father in particular, decided to make trouble for the cops."

I was on a roll now. I was wondering if this performance would ever win me an award.

I'd have to check with Carson if I ever saw him again.

"So what?" Farrell's throat muscles tightened as he struggled to keep an even tone. "That's my right."

"Maybe," I said, "but it made me wonder why."

Silence from behind the big man's desk.

"So I started digging," I said. "And I think I found out."

"I don't care what you think," Farrell snapped.

"Oh, I'm pretty sure you will. Turns out you're chain of dealerships is doing pretty good. Your company's far in the black and your credit rating's higher than I'll probably ever see in my lifetime."

"And the fact I'm well-off means what exactly?"

I flipped another page in my notebook. By now I was on blank pages, but he didn't know that.

"But it turns out you weren't always doing quite as well, were you, Mr. Farrell?"

"I don't know what you mean."

I glanced down at the blank notepaper for a moment. I thought about silently mouthing some words, but that would probably be overdoing it.

I should definitely hit up John Carson, once the feds found him, about skipping the reality show and making me a bona fide actor.

"What I mean," I said, "is you're pretty much a typical third-generation rich guy."

"I don't know what . . ."

"The first generation makes the money; the second generation grows the money; and the third loses it."

Farrell placed his palms flat on his desk and began to push himself up.

"Mark," I said, figuring we'd been talking long enough now I could be informal, "you make a move on me and you're going to find yourself halfway through your wall."

He stayed in his half upright position for a moment before sinking back down into his seat. "How much do you know?" he said.

I grinned. "Now that's more like it. I know you inherited a thriving business from your dad. I know that between all sorts of plans to expand, you know, prove yourself more of a man than the old man was, you came perilously near to losing it all. And I've even come across strong indications that now and then you had to take out loans from some, shall we say, less than upright citizens."

I stopped for a moment and gave him the most piercing look I possibly could. He was fixated on me, tightly enough he appeared to be barely breathing.

"And I know," I continued, "that about four years ago, suddenly you were back in the black and your bankers and creditors were happy for the first time in a long time."

"All of which means what?" he said through gritted teeth.

"All of which means that I've got a pretty good idea where your son and his friends got their dope from. You care to confirm or deny?"

Several long seconds drug by before Farrell spoke up again. "Okay, that's what you know. How about what you want?"

I smiled my third beaming smile of the day. "Now you're talking, buddy."

CHAPTER THIRTY-NINE

L EAVING FARRELL'S DEALERSHIP, AS I FIRED up the Cherokee I remembered I'd put my phone on mute before walking in. I checked for messages, hoping to hear something from Hendricks but nothing yet.

Not quite ten minutes later, I was heading down Arena Avenue, intending to check in at the gym before seeing if the cops had managed to track down Carson when I noticed a silver Lexus with smoked windows a few car lengths behind me.

Smoked windows really only work when you have them rolled up, which made me assume Sean O'Flaherty wanted me to see him sitting in the back seat.

I kept driving and pulled in at the first parking lot I came to. The Lexus pulled in behind me. I got out of the Cherokee and ambled over.

"You may not want to be seen with me at the moment, Sean. I had a sit-down with a fed earlier today."

O'Flaherty grinned and gestured toward the other side of the car. "Climb in, Sam. We've got some more talking to do."

For a moment, I hesitated. I didn't know of any reason why he'd want to do a number on me. After all, we'd left on good terms only that morning, but in the circles O'Flaherty moved in alliances could shift in nothing flat.

"I'm here as an act of charity, Sam. No harm, no foul intended. Besides, if I wanted to hurt you, Paulie here," he gestured towards his driver, a youngish-looking guy with thick dark hair and wearing a leather jacket that strained at the shoulders, "would have already put you down."

Who was I to fight that kind of logic? I climbed into the car, and Paulie pulled out of the parking lot, made a left turn and headed north on Arena.

I had a hunch we were headed out of town, which would only take a few minutes.

"So what can I do for you, Sean?" I asked.

O'Flaherty frowned, but more at life in general than at me. "Something kind of screwy going on, Sam. At the moment, I'm not too involved, and my main concern is that I stay that way."

"If you're using the word screwy, then it must have something to do with John Carson."

O'Flaherty nodded. "Not all that big of a leap, man. Especially considering he's at the center of a mess going on."

"I'm guessing something has changed since this morning?"

"You tell me," the gangster asked.

I sighed. "Sean, you're about the most plugged-in guy in town. Which makes me believe that, even though it only happened a few hours ago you're probably aware someone snatched him."

O'Flaherty chuckled. "Right out from under your nose, the way I hear it."

I grimaced. "Wish I could argue with you, but I can't. But even knowing you the way I do, I'm kind of amazed you already found out. Hell, I don't even know if Special Agent Hendricks has told the cops yet."

"Maybe I've got better sources of information than the locals," O'Flaherty said.

"Maybe." I looked out the window. We'd turned east onto I-70, which definitely meant we were going out of town, right back in the direction I'd just come from. No one at all familiar with the Providence area uses the interstate to get around town during the day.

"Those sources would have to be damned good."

O'Flaherty grinned at me, but I thought the grin looked a little forced.

I continued staring out the window. The Interstate at this time of day, especially since the state keeps putting off turning it six-lane, can be a nightmare, but Paulie navigated his way through with little to no effort on his part.

"Where we going, Sean? You aren't taking me out in the woods or anything are you?"

O'Flaherty shook his head. "Looking for a little privacy, that's all. Someone wants to talk to you."

If I hadn't been so tough and manly, my skin would have started to crawl. It sure felt like a modern-day version of the old-fashioned gangster rides, but despite his profession I'd never known O'Flaherty to be devious.

A minute later we'd crested past the city line, and shortly after passed Farrell Toyota. I wondered if Mark Farrell was still in his office.

We kept going, and within another couple of minutes, Paulie flipped his signal for a right turn.

We came up onto an exit, which Paulie took, turning right almost immediately to catch an access road that at that point runs several miles on either side of the Interstate.

"If you're going to do a number on me," I said, "you may want to find a slightly more private place. Notice all the cars whizzing past us on the highway?"

"Actually, this would be a perfect place to do it," O'Flaherty said. "All those people are going by at over sixty miles an hour, their radios going, eyes half focused on their phones, you think anyone's even aware of what's going on on this side road?"

"You've got a point there," I said.

"But don't worry, Sam. It's nothing like that."

"Good to know."

"I think," he said.

O'Flaherty's kept his expression smooth enough it was impossible to tell if he was kidding or not.

The Lexus pulled into a parking lot shared by an antique mall and a furniture outlet.

A black Cadillac Escalade with darkened windows sat at the far end of the lot across from us.

Two bruiser types in dark suits and sunglasses stood alongside the Caddy, their hands crossed in front of their waists.

Paulie pulled the Lexus to within about ten feet of the other vehicle.

I looked at my host. "Seriously, Sean? A black Caddy?"

O'Flaherty grinned. "What can I say? Some guys are suckers for tradition, even if they do have to upgrade now and then."

Something cold settled into my gut. "Sean, who's in the car?"

His grin vanished as quick as it had come. "I'm guessing you have a pretty good idea, Sam. The man wanted to talk to you, and I said I'd arrange it."

"A phone call wouldn't have worked?" I asked.

"Like I said, he's old-fashioned. And phones, especially nowadays, are way too easy to access."

"So he hopped on a plane just to come see me? I'm guessing he didn't drive all the way this quickly."

"Best not to keep him waiting, Sam. As far as I know he's in a good mood, but you don't want to push it. And when you get right down to it, neither do I."

"Those two goons going to let me inside his car?" I asked.

"Of course."

I turned and looked full on at O'Flaherty. "They going to let me back out again?"

"I'd guess that depends on how your talk goes."

"That's comforting," I said.

"Look at it this way, Sam. If anything bad was going to happen to you, you really think he'd be within a hundred miles of here?"

"Good point," I said, "but how do you all know the feds aren't tracking me? For all you know, they may be all around waiting to pounce."

"I guess that's the chance he's taking. Christ, Sam, quit busting my balls, okay? Just go talk to the guy."

Not seeing much of an option at the moment, I opened my door and got out. Taking a couple of deep breaths, I walked over to the Cadillac. As I got within two feet, one of the black-suited men stepped aside and opened the rear passenger door.

Mentally cursing the day John Carson had come into my gym and gotten me involved in all this, I stooped and climbed in the back seat.

As I settled myself, the man already there spoke up.

"Thank you for coming," he said. "This won't take long."

"Not a problem. Take your time," I said as I settled in opposite the Mafia boss of Chicago.

CHAPTER FORTY

"**Y**OU KNOW WHO I AM?" THE old man asked.
"I do."

Lou Di Maglia was one of the last of the old, old-time mobsters. Compared to him, most of the made men running around these days were toddlers, and even back in his day Gotti had ranked as a teenager next to Di Maglia. There were probably no more than a handful of these guys left, the ones who'd been around in the glory days of the 70's and 80's, before RICO and new immigrant gangs had begun trying to drive the old mob out.

Despite the black Caddy, Di Maglia didn't look any too impressive, which was what made him as dangerous as he was and went a long way to explaining why he'd lasted as long as he had. Unlike some wise guys, who strutted around in a way to make sure everyone knew who they were, Di Maglia was more like his generation, the Gambino's and Castellano's who had done their best to stay low key and out of the public light.

Somewhere down the line, Di Maglia had pretty much inherited the Chicago area. I'd never been out that way much, but while wrestling for the Midwest Wrestling League out of St. Louis I'd bounced around most of Missouri and Illinois, and I'd been in enough dives and shady arenas, dealt with enough gamblers and fixers of various kinds, that I'd often brushed up against his name and reputation.

There'd been a long stretch of time where St. Louis, primarily in the form of Don Lipardo, had pretty much controlled the middle and eastern parts of the state. However, in the last few years Chicago had been making more and more of a claim on the area, leaving the St. Louis mob pretty much twiddling their thumbs on the sidelines.

The man sitting across from me wasn't exactly what I had pictured. He was old, sure. If the man had been active in the Outfit back in the 70's, he would have to be far past his prime. But I'd always kind of expected a guy, even in his old age, full of vim and vigor, and that wasn't the picture presented here.

Di Maglia was on the smallish side, even accounting for the natural shrinkage that comes with old age and even in his youth probably hadn't topped five eight, and obviously he was much smaller now. He wore a light tan topcoat, but I could tell there wasn't a whole lot of meat, if there ever had been any, left on his bones. His face was drawn in and puckered, with wattles on his neck, and liver spots on both hands.

He had only a few wispy strands of hair, almost gone and completely gray.

However, looking in his eyes, you could tell you didn't want to cross this feeble old man. The eyes were either dark brown or black, for some reason I couldn't quite tell which, and they had a flat, dull aspect, like the eyes of a snake.

After the initial introductions, we sat and stared at each other for a minute.

"You know why I came all this way?" Di Maglia asked.

"Considering I can't think of any other reason, I assume it has something to do with my client and his dead partner."

The mob boss nodded. "Your client is this goofball from Hollywood?"

"Yeah," I said, "for lack of a better term you could call him my client. And goofball does describe him pretty well."

For an instant, Di Maglia's lips quirked. "Are you trying to solve his partner's murder?"

"Sort of. I'm kind of leaving that to the cops while I try to keep him in one piece."

"And figure out what's going on?" the old man croaked.

"Yeah," I said. "And figure out what's going on."

"I hear that he's vanished. That you left him alone for a few minutes and someone took him."

"Yeah." I grimaced. "That's pretty much how it happened."

Di Maglia stared at me for a moment. Up to now, things had gone about as smoothly as could be expected, considering the circumstances. But I couldn't for an instant forget that, despite, his age, I was sitting across from one of the most dangerous men in the country.

After a moment, the old man gave me a short nod. "I've been speaking over the course of the last day with various people, business acquaintances, both direct and indirect. Most of them from the West Coast."

"Okay," I said.

"They assure me, to a man, they have nothing to do with this woman's death."

"Forgive my disrespect," I said, "but would any of them have reason to lie to you?"

The mobster grinned. "Many of them would have reason to lie. But I don't think any of them would dare."

"You saying none of them knew she was about to turn herself in to the feds?" I asked.

"One or two told me they had faint suspicions, but nothing firm enough to act on. At least not yet."

I mulled that one over. "The cops are pretty sure that's the reason for her being killed."

Di Maglia snorted. "And how experienced are these cops? This is, after all, a fairly small town."

I took a deep breath, feeling like I was tiptoeing through a mine field. "One of them's William Santiago."

Di Maglia blinked but kept his expression neutral. "Of course. I'd forgotten he came out here after he left Chi."

I took a deep breath and felt like I was looking down the side of a forty-story building. "Mind telling me how a man of your importance knows the name of a mere police lieutenant?"

Di Maglia grinned. "Yes, I do mind. Let's just say that with men like young William around, your town's probably in better hands than it deserves."

I'd never myself considered Santiago as "young," but figured to a man of Di Maglia's age everyone else looked like a pup.

"A couple of people on our city council would disagree with you," I said.

"Regardless," the old guy continued, "while my knowledge couldn't be considered as evidence or proof, I can assure you, with certainty, none of Miss Truell's clients were responsible for her death or your friend's disappearance."

"I hate to disagree with you," I said. "But a couple of them attacked me the other day."

The old mobster nodded. "You sure about that?" he asked.

I blinked. "That I got attacked?"

"No, that the people involved were sent by Miss Truell's clients."

"It feels like a fairly safe assumption," I said.

"Have they identified your attackers?"

"Yes."

"And have they connected them to any – unsavory elements?"

I paused. "Not that I know of. But the cops don't share everything with me."

"I received word on this situation yesterday," Di Maglia said.

"Word?"

The old mobster nodded. "The other night there was an informal meeting out west of—interested parties."

"Okay."

"And these parties, after much discussion, decided to quietly divorce themselves from the situation, rather than throw good energy and motion after bad."

"When was this decision made?" I asked.

"A far as I can tell, it was two days ago. Once all the parties agreed, they reached out to me to smooth things over here as much as possible."

"Makes sense, I guess," I said. "If you don't mind me asking, were you one of Miss Truell's clients?"

For an instant, barely a fraction of a second, something flared behind those cold, dark eyes. My skin tightened, as I wondered if my question had somehow crossed a point of no return.

But in the next instant, Di Maglia's eyes returned to their original blankness. "I'm showing you some leeway, Mr. Quinton, partly because you're not part of our world and partly because my local colleague has some fondness for you. I'm going to answer your question, but you are to never again, in any way, shape, or form, inquire into my business affairs. Ever. Understood?"

"Understood," I said as I began breathing again.

"The answer is no. Not only does my—organization—have its own people to provide those services, we would never trust somebody we didn't know, and control, intimately."

"Fair enough," I said. "So you're here more in the capacity of an elder statesman, a goodwill ambassador?"

The old guy pondered that one for a moment. "Yes," he said. "That's a good way to put it. I'm simply a goodwill ambassador. But the goodwill part is conditional."

"The condition being leaving your friends and business associates alone?" I asked.

Di Maglia nodded. "You assume correctly, Mr. Quinton. Do you have any more questions before Mr. O'Flaherty takes you back home?"

"Just one," I said, "but I doubt you can answer it. If none of your associates are in town, who the hell snatched my client, and who the hell was gunning for us yesterday?"

"I've no idea. I only know it wasn't my people. Beyond that, Mr. Detective, I guess you'll have to figure out on your own, huh?"

One thing about the old boy. I couldn't fault his logic.

CHAPTER FORTY-ONE

"**Y**OU HAD A SIT-DOWN WITH WHO?" Josh Nichols asked me half an hour later.

We were sitting in Santiago's office, and the lieutenant himself was there as well. I'd called Nichols almost as soon as I'd left the meeting with the don and strongly urged him to find Santiago and get him into the office as well.

Nichols had pointed out his boss was under an informal suspension, and I'd emphasized the "informal" part of that. We dickered back and forth for a while before he asked me to give him twenty minutes before I showed up.

When I arrived, they were both in the head man's office, looking at me with varying degrees of suspicion as I walked in.

The dynamic in the office was kind of strange. Santiago, wearing slacks and a black guayabera shirt that no doubt, as with most of his wardrobe, cost more than the average person's car payment, was sitting in a chair off to the side while Nichols sat behind his lieutenant's desk.

"I said I had a meeting with Lou Di Maglia, the boss of Chicago." I looked straight at Santiago. "He says hi by the way."

The lieutenant frowned, but didn't say anything in response.

Nichols glanced at his boss, then back to me. "What did he want?"

I gave them the gist of the conversation Di Maglia and I had had. When I was done, I sat back and waited for a response.

"Well of course he'd say that," Nichols said. "He's a crook. You didn't expect him to confess, did you?"

"Not the way it works," Santiago said. "You're right, that Di Maglia's as crooked as they come. But he's telling the truth here."

"What makes you say that?" Nichols asked, looking at his boss.

"Because otherwise there'd be no reason for him to pick Sam up. What does he have to gain by mixing in with whatever little shit storm's going on in Providence? It's a pretty safe bet Miss Truell's client list didn't include any of the Italian boys, at least not of the Midwestern variety, so what the hell does he care?"

"It's causing a little heat for his man on the scene," I pointed out.

Santiago shrugged. "A little, but nothing that won't blow over in no time."

"You're saying he had nothing to gain by mixing himself into this," Nichols said.

Santiago nodded. "Exactly. If he was guilty of anything, why pop up out of the blue and bring attention to himself? Especially with Hendricks and his bunch circling around. And if he's not guilty, what does it hurt to take half a day to travel out here, talk to the man at the center of it all, then go home? Not much of a hassle to ease up some temporary heat that won't amount to much anyway."

"You think you can trust a hood like that?" Nichols asked.

"Doesn't matter," Santiago said. "Di Maglia's old school."

"Old school meaning he believes in honor, family, and all that crap? Come on, boss. You don't really buy that do you?"

"Not that," Santiago said. "Old school in terms of if he thought someone was out of line on his turf, he'd send in a squad of hoods, and we'd have a full-on gang war going on right now. The fact we don't, means we can trust what he says."

"Which leaves us right where we were before," I said. "Any trace of Carson at all?"

"Not yet," Nichols said. "But not for lack of trying on our part. We've got the word out and are working it from our end, and the feds are scouring the town up one side and down the other."

"Sounds like you're each playing your own side of the field."

Nichols grinned. "If by that you mean the federal boys and girls don't trust us hicks a whole lot, you'd be right. But on something like this, we're showing each other at least nominal support."

"Yet no sign of him. No word from any of your street level sources?"

"You kidding, Blondie. Street level sources? In Providence?" Nichols said.

"Right. You guys are flying blind all the time, right?"

"Well, okay, then, maybe we do have some extra ears out on this one, seeing as we're talking a homicide and all."

"Doesn't that strike you as a little odd, Josh?"

"You mean that, considering how small this city is, all the cops, federals, and informers can't find a trace of an out-of-towner who, let's be frank, doesn't have a whole lot of smarts?"

"That's what I mean."

"Yeah," Nichols said. "Something seems off, and it's making us feel kind of stupid, you know?"

"Unless you look at the other possibility."

"Which is?" Nichols asked.

Santiago spoke up. "That Carson's already left town."

"Yeah," Nichols said, "we thought about that one too. Made a call to L.A., and they're going to keep an eye on all of his known places for a while. But I've got a hunch that says he's still somewhere local. A guy with so little street smarts can't hardly unzip his fly without announcing it to the world."

I looked out the inner window of Santiago's office for a moment. At this time of the day, about half the detectives had gone home, and the skeleton night shift hadn't shown up yet. Something about the empty desks and absence of motion got to me.

"Has it also occurred to you guys," I asked after a few minutes, "that none of this adds up in any way?"

"'Course it has," Nichols said. "Guy comes to town to make a TV show about you."

"First thing that doesn't make sense," Santiago said. I thought of sticking out my tongue at him but didn't want to spend the night in jail.

"His business partner," Nichols continued as if his informally-suspended lieutenant hadn't spoken, "comes along, and even though it's unusual he doesn't think twice about it. She wants to wait till she gets all the way out here to turn herself in to witness protection."

"Which means," I interrupted, "that she'd already reached out to them. How many times you know those guys to let civilians set the ground rules?"

"Hardly ever," Nichols said. "Then no sooner do the two of them hit town then she winds up dead."

"Ain't that convenient for us," Santiago grunted.

"And before you know it her partner's in the wind and we can't track him down. Did I leave anything out?" Nichols asked.

"How about the two gun battles I was involved in?"

"I meant did I leave anything relevant out."

"Probably," I said, "but it's hurting my brain to try to keep it all straight."

"Then go home," Santiago said. "You've had quite the day anyway. It's not every day you get to meet someone like Lou Di Maglia."

"Good enough," I said, "but there is one other thing."

Both cops looked at me.

I reached into my jacket and pulled out a micro tape cassette. I flicked it to Nichols., who caught it automatically.

"You may want to listen to that," I said. I looked straight at Santiago. "Both of you may want to listen to it."

"What is it?" Nichols asked.

"Conversation I had earlier with Mark Farrell."

Santiago half rose from his chair, his eyes narrowed. "What about?"

I grinned, hoping to defuse the sudden tension. "I was looking for common ground with him on behalf of my client."

"Your client?" Nichols asked. "What client?"

"I guess clients would be more accurate. The parents of one of his son's accomplices."

Santiago eased himself back down. "And I'm guessing because of the old client confidentiality bit you couldn't tell him who you were working for."

"Yeah," I said. "We argued about it a bit, but I wore him down eventually. Listen to the tape, guys. I'm happy to authenticate it if it comes to that, but I'm guessing it won't."

I got up and headed to the door.

"Sam," Nichols said.

I turned. "Yeah?"

"You let us know if Carson gets ahold of you, right?"

"Sure, but what makes you think he'll reach out to me?"

"Far as we know, you're the only friend he has in the area."

I grinned. "Don't know if I'd call him a friend. Hell, he hasn't even made me a star yet."

CHAPTER FORTY-TWO

I SPENT THE NIGHT WITH TALIA, DOING my best not to think of the week's events, and about three thirty the next morning my phone rang.

I eased myself across her, she hadn't woken up to the sound, reached down, and snagged my phone out of my jeans pocket.

"Yeah," I whispered into it.

"Fredericks Park," Josh Nichols said. "Something you may want to see."

The cops wanting to show me something this early in the morning didn't sound good, but I hung up without saying anything else and went about getting myself dressed in the dark as quietly as I could.

Managing to sneak out without waking my sleeping friend, I got in the Cherokee and headed towards Fredericks.

Fredericks Park is right about in the center of Providence, abutting on the southern edge of the downtown area, and it has a worse reputation than it deserves. Most people in the surrounding towns know of the park because it's often described by the news people as the scene of numerous shootings, assaults, and other assorted mayhems.

The truth as the locals see it, though, is a bit different. While Fredericks, with its central location and proximity to residential areas, does see its share of crime, I've lost count of the number of times I've heard TV reporters breathlessly give Fredericks as the scene of the latest outrage, only for the actual location to be any-where from a block to, in one case I remember, ten blocks away from the park itself.

Not this time, though. As I came along the western edge of the park, I saw the assortment of flashing lights, both cop and ambu-lance, that I'd feared.

I pulled into a far corner of the parking lot, got out, and walked over to see what there was to see.

My chest felt a little tight. The only reason I could see for Nichols to call me out was John Carson, but as I got up close, I saw both Nichols and Santiago standing over a crumpled body on the park's basketball court.

Santiago was in what for him would be considered half dress. He was wearing a dark suit with a gray dress shirt, but missing a tie.

For somebody supposed to be off duty, he was spending an awful lot of time around departmental activity.

The usual assortment of crime scene people were moving around doing their usual assortment of stuff, including a number of uniformed cops standing around looking for something to do, the ambulance pulled up about fifty feet away, two EMT's sitting on the bumper waiting to be told to haul something off.

They reminded me a lot of the EMT's from the shootout the day before.

As I came alongside of the scene, I started breathing easier. The body on the ground definitely wasn't Carson's.

It was a younger man. Hard to tell with half his head blown away, but probably no more than twenty-five. The body was lean and in the overhead court lights looked a little undernourished.

Again, though, hard to be sure in the condition he was in.

Santiago looked at me. "Know him?" he asked.

I glanced at one of the crime scene techs, who nodded, and I knelt down to get a closer look.

After a minute, I shook my head and stood up. "Never seen him before," I said.

"You're sure?" Santiago asked, an odd tone in his voice.

"As sure as I can be," I said. "I may have passed him on the street at some point, or he may be a client at the gym I see every now and then. But at the moment, the face doesn't ring a bell. Who is he?"

Nichols glanced down at a notebook in his hand. "Name on his license says Frank Weatherly."

"Sorry, Lieutenant, Don't know the guy. Before I get too cranky and we all start yelling at each other, how about telling me why you hauled me out here?"

The two cops looked at each other, and Santiago nodded.

Nichols reached down and brought out a plastic evidence bag for me to see.

The bag held what looked like a driver's license.

I squinted at it in the partial illumination from the park lights.

"That's not a Missouri license," I said after a moment.

"Nope," Nichols said. "California."

I glanced down again at the still form of the young man on the ground. "California," I said.

"Los Angeles County, to be precise," Santiago said.

"Got a town yet?" I asked.

"Not at the moment, but we put in a request. Doesn't matter at the moment, the county alone tells us quite a bit."

"But not enough," I said.

"No, not enough. Except we've got an influx of people from California in town this week, and they all seem to end up either dead or missing."

"We put a call in to rush things along," Nichols said, "but it's still the middle of the night out there."

"You give Hendricks a heads up?" I asked.

"Sure. One way or another, our guess is this is all connected."

"Yeah," I said, "but connected how? This guy doesn't look like a gangbanger or anything. He looks like a beach bum."

"I'm sure you've caught on," Santiago said, "that he looks an awful lot like the guys that've been glomming on to you and your buddy Carson."

I nodded. "Blond, tanned. This one looks a little skinnier, but other than that, these guys could darned near be clones of each other."

"Last I heard," Santiago said, "there isn't any organized crime family made up of handsome blonds."

"Have you gotten ID's yet on the three who ambushed us in the hotel?" I asked.

Santiago nodded at Nichols, who took out his phone, tapped something up on the screen, and began reading. "Just came through earlier this evening. John Andrews, 26, bartender, Torrance. Harry Johnson, 24, Studio City, personal trainer. And Lance Jackson, I swear that's his real name, 29, Culver City, made his living mainly as a delivery guy."

Something niggled in the back of my head. "Isn't it unusual for gunmen to have workaday jobs like that?" I asked.

"Not really," Santiago said. "You wouldn't know it from the movies, but most of these guys live hand to mouth. And even the successful ones have some sort of legitimate employment on the books. Mainly for the IRS."

It still felt off. I felt like all I needed was one little thing to click into place, and it would all make sense.

The three of us stepped back out of the way and let the tech people do their thing. I really didn't need to hang around there, but I didn't yet feel like going back home.

After a few minutes of silence on our part, Santiago spoke up. "We listened to the recording you gave us," he said.

"Uh huh."

"Nothing there that can be used in court."

"No," I said. "But that wasn't really the point."

"I didn't think so. First thing tomorrow, I'm going to have a talk with Councilman Farrell."

"You going to tell him he's a suspect in a major heroin ring?" I asked.

"Maybe. We'll see how it plays out. We're also going to start digging into the backgrounds of the other kids' parents."

I nodded. "My guess is they weren't all in on it. Hard to keep something like that secret, after all. But I'd lay it safe odds at least one or two others had partnered up with Farrell."

"What got you onto it?" Nichols asked.

"Simple. I looked into the man's financial background. Found out that up to a few years back, his whole business was about to go under. Then it began righting itself."

Santiago shook his head. "I figured the guy for a typical blow-hard politician. But to find out he was using his own kid as a mule for his dope business, geez."

Nichols shook his head. "So all his storm and fury about his poor son being ramrodded by the cops . . ."

"Was just cover," I said. "He was really worried you guys were getting close to him."

"Which we weren't," Santiago said. "Hell, we didn't even have a clue."

"Weird you got him to admit all this," Nichols said.

A couple of men in coveralls came by lugging some arc lights set on tripods. Once they moved past us, they began setting the lights up on opposite sides of the crime scene. Snapping on the lights caused the area to blaze like crazy. One of the techs examining something about five feet from the body looked up and flashed an okay sign.

"You may want to listen to the tape again, Josh. Farrell didn't actually admit to everything. We basically talked in circles the whole time."

"There's enough for probable cause, though," Santiago said. "And that's what I'm going to snap in his face first thing in the morning." He arched an eyebrow at me. "You did pretty good, Quinton. Even without saying it flat out, anyone listening in would have naturally assumed you were working for one of his partners."

I nodded. "But because they were keeping everything pretty much hush-hush, I didn't need to even name who my 'client' was."

Because there didn't seem anything left to say, the three of us went back to staring at the crime scene and wondering who Frank Weatherly was.

Eventually, the photo guys finished up and nodded to the head crime scene guy, who in turn made a motion to the EMT's to cart the body away.

"Might as well pack it in," Santiago said. "None of us are doing much here except getting in the way."

Nichols nodded, but for some reason we didn't move. After a moment, Nichols spoke up.

"It's goddamned confusing," he said. "Witness protection, three million dollars missing, blond surfer dudes running around town shooting up everything they see. It's like a script from some godawful straight-to-video movie."

Click.

"Christ," I said.

The two cops turned to look at me.

"What?" Nichols asked.

"A bartender, a personal trainer, and a delivery man."

"Yeah?"

Santiago arched an eyebrow. I had a feeling he was following my lead.

"And the two from the car wash were security guards."

"What are you getting at, Sam?" Nichols asked.

"These guys, Josh. They're not gangsters or cartel guys in any way. They're actors."

"Actors?"

"Yeah. I'll bet if you dig a little deeper you'll find they all act on the side from their regular jobs. And I bet you'll find the same with this one they just carted away. Hell, he even looked like a starving artist."

"Actors," Santiago said.

"Right. And they're following a script."

The two cops took a moment to digest it. "Question is," Nichols finally asked, "if they're following a script, who wrote it?"

I shook my head at him. "Do you really have to ask?"

CHAPTER FORTY-THREE

NICHOLS CALLED SEVEN HOURS LATER. I was in my office at the gym, working on the computer, a full-page portrait that I'd printed off in front of me on my desk.

"Frank Weatherly is an actor," Nichols said by way of greeting.

"I know."

"How do you know?" Nichols asked. "You get some of your mob friends to run him down?"

"Friend," I said, "as in singular. And I'm not sure O'Flaherty would describe me and him as friends."

"Good to know."

"Yeah," I said, "but that's not what I did. I'm sitting in the office at my computer. Ever hear of Google?"

Nichols sighed, and I could hear fatigue in the sound. More than likely, after looking down at Weatherly's body in the park he hadn't been able to go back home and to bed for a few hours as I had. "Sometimes the simplest ways are the easiest. Maybe one day us dumb cops will figure that out."

"Maybe," I said. "What'd you find out the old-fashioned way?"

"Kid was twenty-two years old, originally from Pierre, South Dakota. Played basketball in college for one year before he came down wrong on a play and tore up his knee. Drifted into some modeling gigs, and in no time at all headed for sunny California to find his fame and fortune."

"You ever hear of him before last night?" I asked.

"Nope."

"So much for fame."

"Hell, he was only 22. Who knows what could have been?"

"Actually, I've got an idea of what was. If you haven't already, pull up his IMDb page and see what you find."

I waited as faintly over the phone coming the tapping of keys. After about a minute and half, Nichols whistled in my ear. "Son of a bitch," he said.

"Yep. Would you take any money at all to call it a coincidence?"

"Kid's got a mighty thin list, no more than eight guest roles in a couple of soap operas and a handful of commercials."

"Uh huh," I said.

"But he did have an eight-episode run on a reality show called *Three for a Party.*"

"Yep," I said, "produced by none other than Monumental Productions and your friend and mine John Carson."

"Give me a minute," Nichols said.

I waited for more than a minute, actually closer to five, before he came back on the line. "Okay, I didn't take time to go through all of them, but I looked over the credits on three of our other bozos."

"I'll bet I can tell you what you found," I said.

"Let me guess. You've already looked up the others."

"Right," I said.

"Why didn't you tell me first and save me five minutes?" Nichols asked.

"Hey, buddy. I'm a taxpayer. I want to see civil servants work occasionally."

"At least four of these yahoos, these West Coast hitmen, had parts on Carson's TV shows."

"Actually five," I said.

"We need to find Carson," Nichols said.

"That we do."

CHAPTER FORTY-FOUR

A FTER JOSH AND I HUNG UP, I sat at my desk in deep thought. When nothing came to me after a few minutes, I started drumming my fingers, hoping to spark something.

The drumming was a good call because about ninety seconds later a great idea popped into my head.

At least, I thought it was a great idea. It had been so long since I'd had one I wasn't entirely sure.

After another minute or two of what, for me, passes for deep thinking, nothing better had emerged. I picked up the phone and called Talia Sanderson.

"You've got exactly five minutes," she said. "I'm at work, and in six minutes, I'm expected in the chancellor's office for a meeting."

"At work on a Saturday? What happened to the sacred academic weekend? You know, the one that starts on Thursday afternoon and goes until lunchtime Tuesday?"

"This particular sacred weekend falls only a few weeks into the semester, meaning everyone's still piled to the gills around here. Like I said, even the chancellor's in his office and waiting for me."

"Did you have a professor get lost on the way to his class?" I asked.

"No."

"Having a discussion on whether to require students to take at least one test to actually pass their classes?"

"Keep it up, Sam, and whenever we're in public I'll start calling you Blondie every chance I get."

I grinned and leaned back in my chair. There had been a time, back in my younger days when I was still wrestling, when I had no problem with the shortened form of my stage name, The Blond Bomber. Especially when it was being shouted out by frantic female fans.

But it seems the older I get the more I find myself shaking my head at the silliness of youth.

"How about we change the subject?" I said.

"Only if it's something that can be handled in four minutes or less. The chancellor's not a guy who likes to be kept waiting."

"Not even if you were on the phone with your snookums?" I asked.

"Three and a half minutes now, snookums."

"Fair enough," I said. "I need to speak with someone in your theatre department."

"You may have forgotten, but I'm dean of social sciences, not fine arts."

"I know, but I figured you would know someone who knows someone who knows someone."

"It's possible," Talia said. "When I get out of my meeting. Looking for anyone in particular?"

"Someone more on the acting side of things, and if possible someone with some experience in TV or movies."

"In other words, hooray for Hollywood?"

"That's the idea," I said.

"This have anything to do with the fact you snuck out of my place in the wee hours of the morning?"

"I obviously wasn't sneaky enough," I said.

"If by sneaky you mean being anything less than a rampaging elephant, no you weren't."

"Short answer to your question, though, is yes. It does have something to do with that."

"I heard something on the radio this morning about a body found in the park."

"Yeah?"

"Yeah. Is that by chance where you stormed out to?"

"If by stormed you mean tiptoed delicately, yeah pretty much."

Talia giggled. "Considering our geographic location, I doubt our department is the most tied in to Hollywood and all that, but I'm thinking of a couple of people who may fit that bill. Okay if I call you back in a couple of hours?"

"Sure," I said. "I'll be here at the gym trying to make it look like I work for a living."

"As opposed to university types like me who only sit in meetings all day?"

I grinned. "Don't forget you make phone calls to help out your boyfriend as well."

"Uh huh," Talia said. "Got to go."

She hung up. I had a few hours to kill and figured, though I'd been joking, maybe it wouldn't hurt to go out into the main area of the gym and actually do some honest work for a while.

CHAPTER FORTY-FIVE

Talia came through as I knew she would, and I met Emily Brown that afternoon at a coffee shop in the university's student union.

She had arrived first and already had a table, not much of a feat on a weekend. When I entered I made a straight line for her. She was reading something on an iPad while sipping from a small cup.

I didn't see any foam, cream, or caramel around her mouth and wondered if she was drinking actual coffee in a coffee shop.

Unheard of.

"Dr. Brown," I said.

She looked up and took a minute to give me a good going over. "It's Professor Brown, not doctor. I only have an MFA. Mr. Quinton, I'm guessing."

"Yeah, mind if I sit?"

Gesturing me to an empty chair, she put the iPad away in her purse. "There's a lot of people in here. How did you know who I was?"

"Dr. Sanderson told me to look for a young woman who was the exact opposite of what I expected a theatre professor to look like."

She smiled. "I'm not sure if I should take that as a compliment or not."

"Since I'm guessing it's the image you're trying to project, I'd say compliment."

Emily Brown definitely didn't fit the stereotype for a woman theatre teacher. She looked, sitting down, to be about five seven with long straight black hair and light brown eyes. She was wearing a gray silk blazer with black slacks and a maroon blouse with two buttons open.

Not a Birkenstock or plaid wool skirt anywhere in sight.

"Compliment it is then. For what it's worth, she told me to keep an eye out for someone who looked like a bouncer."

"Made it pretty easy to pick me out, huh?"

Professor Brown grinned, then shook her head a bit. "So what can I do for you?"

"I need some information on the performance community here in Providence."

"What kind of information? Dr. Sanderson didn't tell me much about what this concerned."

"What did she say?"

"That you were a private investigator working on some sort of case and needed a little background."

"That was enough to make you willing to give up your afternoon?" I asked.

Emily smiled. "It also gave me a reason to skip rehearsal for our upcoming play."

"And that's a good thing?"

She paused to take a drink from her cup. "Ordinarily, no. But as the second director, I'm getting a bit bushed. We open in three weeks, and we're nowhere near ready."

"What's the second director do?" I asked.

Another drink, then she put the cup down. "Everything the director doesn't want to mess with. This close to opening, it's like herding lions instead of cats."

"May I ask why you're only second director?"

"You may, and the answer's simple. Because I'm only an assistant professor."

It could have come off as bitter or self-pitying, but instead she simply stated things as if "this is the way of the world and nothing to worry about."

"But we're here to talk about your issue, aren't we? Why do you want to know about the theatre scene here in town?"

"Cards on the table?" I asked.

"Please."

"I'm investigating a murder, actually two of them, plus assorted other crimes, and I'm also looking for my client, who's gone missing."

Emily Brown put an elbow on the table, held her arm vertically, and placed her chin in her palm. "Was the young man killed in the park last night one of them?" she asked.

"That was quick," I said. "And yes."

"Not all that quick. Although I'm in fine arts, I do stay up on local events of all sorts."

"Plus, since Providence isn't exactly St. Louis when it comes to violent crime, you didn't have a lot of homicides to choose from."

"No, but there seems to have been quite a lot of violence in the news the last few days. I'm also going to go out on a limb and guess the woman killed in the hotel downtown is the other."

"You do keep up on what's happening," I said.

"Again, not hard to do in a town of our size. But I'm waiting to hear what you want from me."

"The woman you mentioned, Wendy Truell, was a TV producer," I said.

Emily Brown nodded. "I remember hearing that."

"The young man killed in the park last night was an actor."

Her lips pursed, and her brown eyes narrowed. "From around here?"

"No, from California."

"I'm not quite following," she said.

"It's probably no coincidence that two murder victims within a couple days of each other were from the same area and in the same business."

I decided not to confuse the issue by mentioning all the other sometime actors wandering around in this mess.

She nodded, and her eyes widened again. "And you're wondering if there's anyone else in town from with the same connections."

I raised my hand into a toy gun, pointed it at her, and pulled the trigger. "Bingo. Actually, I know for a fact at least one person with similar contacts is somewhere around here, or at least he was up to the other day."

"So you're interested in knowing, if someone from the film world was hanging out around Providence, where would they go to—what—be around like-minded folks?"

I cocked my head at her. "You sure you're an assistant professor? You seem awfully smart to be at that level."

Emily Brown giggled, but in a dignified way. "You think I should be promoted up?"

"Hell no. I was more wondering how you were ever allowed into the academic ranks at all with this ability to put two and two together."

The giggle became a full-out laugh. "I'm going to do you a big favor," she said, "and not mention that comment to Dr. Sanderson."

"I'd appreciate it. She'd probably hack up all my tee-shirts, and I wouldn't have anything to wear."

Another laugh, a little lower register this time, and she reached into her purse, pulling out a small notepad and pen.

"I don't know if this will help," she said as she began writing, "but you're correct in thinking the acting community around here is fairly small and insular. Anyone in the field coming from out of town, even if they were major players, would become known pretty damned quick."

"Would you know about it?" I asked as she capped the pen and replaced it in her purse.

"Possibly," she said, "but I've been working seventy-hour weeks the last month getting this play together and haven't had much time for general smoozing. It would take me a couple of phone calls, but I think I can nail down what you need."

As she spoke, she made some notations on the pad. "Give me an hour or so," she said, "and call me back. I assume you'll need something in the way of a personal introduction as well?'

"Wouldn't hurt," I said, "but don't worry. I'll make sure you come out of this in one piece."

"Could you do me one favor," she asked.

"What's that?"

"Let me know how this all turns out? My boyfriend's trying to break into screenwriting, and I've got the notion there could be an interesting story here. He could maybe even hire you as a consultant of some kind."

"Fair enough," I said.

Emily Brown stood up. "Let me make some phone calls," she said, "and I'll get back to you."

CHAPTER FORTY-SIX

Several hours later, Emily Brown and I were sitting on a bench outside the downtown Starbucks on Main Street when two young men walked up to us. As the Starbucks was closed for the night, we weren't drinking anything.

Around us swirled the usual mix of downtown Providence on a warm, late summer night. Lots of groups, hardly anyone walking alone. Most of the groups had from two to four people, and the average age was probably somewhere around twenty-three. It made me feel conspicuous, but Emily merely leaned back on the bench and soaked it all in.

She nodded in their direction as the two men came up to us.

They looked like carbon copies, both of each other and of Frank Weatherly, the kid found dead in the park. Not to mention of most of the other young actors I'd come across in the last few days.

Medium tall, longish blond hair, blue eyes and slim, though fairly firm builds. They both sported Malibu tans, though I could see a smear of pale under the golden brown.

These guys were nervous.

I had the thought that if I'd been casting a soap opera from the nineties, these were the guys I would go for.

When they got up to the bench, they stopped and looked at us. They were both wearing faded blue jeans and tight tee-shirts, one navy blue and one green.

I was pretty sure, even at my age, tight tee-shirts looked better on me than on these guys.

"You wanted to see us?" the one in green said to Emily. Both of them ignored me and focused on her.

"Are you Lewis and Roy?" she asked.

"Yeah," responded Green Kid. "And you don't need to make it sound like some kind of Vegas show act."

"Sorry," Emily said.

Navy Blue Kid finally looked at me. "This the guy we're supposed to meet?"

"I am," I said.

The two glanced at each other almost as if the two of them shared a single brain. Considering their appearance and attitude, I could believe it.

"We're only here because the people we're staying with like Professor Brown, but we've got things to do. We'll give you five minutes."

I shook my head and rolled my shoulders. I was suddenly tired of show-biz types, whether the real thing or wannabes. "Seen Frank lately?

The two jerked. Navy Blue started to say something, then clamped his mouth shut.

"I'm guessing you haven't, for at least the last twenty hours or so."

"So what?" Green asked. "What's your point?"

"Hear about the body they found in the park this morning? Shot in the head and dead on the ground? Hear about that?"

The paleness beneath their tans increased. Navy Blue began to jitter a bit, as if he wanted to run far away. But I knew they weren't going anywhere until they at least heard the score.

They were too young, too far from home, and in far, far over their heads.

I turned to Emily. "Thanks for your help. But I think my new friends and I can take it from here."

She nodded, stood up, and held out her hand. We shook, and she winked at the two young men before walking away.

"Sit down, guys," I said. "We've got a lot to talk about."

CHAPTER FORTY-SEVEN

"I T WAS SUPPOSED TO BE A practice run," Lewis said a few minutes later. Lewis was the one in the blue shirt. As he spoke, Roy in the green shirt nodded.

"A practice run," I said.

Lewis started nodding now, and I felt like I was looking at two bobble-head dolls. "Right," he said, "for the movie."

"Movie."

"You know," Roy said, "The movie Mr. Carson's producing."

Looking at the two of them, I wondered if I'd ever been that young and naïve.

Probably.

"Tell me about this movie," I said. "What's the basic plot?"

"It's pretty cool," Lewis said. "It's about a TV producer who gets involved with the drug cartels and the Mafia. He tries to turn himself in to the government, but gets kidnapped by the bad guys before he can."

"Yeah," Roy spoke up, "and then his partner gets killed as a warning."

"What happens after that?" I asked.

The two looked at each other before looking down to the ground.

"Actually," Lewis said, "we, uh, never saw the full treatment."

"So what was your part in all this? I'm assuming Frank Weatherly was in town with you to work on this, what'd you call it, dry run?"

"Yeah, Frank. As well as a couple of other guys he brought out here. We were supposed to be the cartel operatives who kidnap the TV producer."

I looked at the two of them. Blond, tanned, blue-eyed and bodies like professional pickleball players. "You guys were planning on playing cartel operatives in this movie?"

"Yeah," Roy said, "we kind of wondered about that ourselves. Like, we don't really fit the profile, you know? But Mr. Carson said a lot of the South American gangs use white guys as operatives. Like camouflage, you know? Besides, we've worked with him before."

"On some of his reality shows."

The two actually looked a bit embarrassed at that.

"Uh huh."

"And because Mr. Carson's a player in the business, we figured he should know."

Something told me the two actors and I didn't exactly define "player" the same way, but it wasn't the time to go into that.

"It's weird, though," Roy said, "because so far we haven't done much of anything but sit around while Mr. Carson's been zooming around working on the deal. We haven't even been rehearsing or anything."

I stared at Roy for a minute. "I think you've done a bit more than that," I aid.

The kid squirmed and looked away.

"Your voice is kind of familiar," I said. "Have we spoken before?"

He looked down at his feet and shook his head.

"You sure?" I asked. "Maybe we spoke on the phone sometime?"

Roy's shoulders slumped, and after a minute he looked back up at me. "Yeah, I was the guy who called you."

"On the disposable phone," I said.

He nodded. "Mr. Carson said it was kind of like a screen test. You know, rehearsing part of the script."

"To what end?"

"He said there was going to be a lot of stuff going on in the story, a lot of ways the bad guys were trying to confuse the good guys and throw them off. But honest, making that call to you was about all we've done. Other than sit around, we haven't had a whole lot to do with the movie yet."

"The other guys have, I think," Lewis piped in.

"Other guys?" I asked.

Lewis nodded. "There was a bunch of us that Mr. Carson brought out here. Some of the others have been staying somewhere else, and Mr. Carson said he's had them rehearsing."

Cannon fodder, I thought. A secondary line in case the real troops couldn't pull it off. Just sitting around waiting to be used and not even knowing it.

"So what happened to Frank?" I asked. "Any ideas?"

The bobble heads stared at each other again before Roy answered. "Frank didn't quite seem like he was going with the program, you know? He was always questioning Mr. Carson, disagreeing with him, you know? And you just don't do that sort of thing with someone who's going to make your career, right?"

"Right," I said. "You know if he and Carson got into it at all?"

Another mutual glance, and in concert their shoulders slumped. I worried if I stayed with them too much longer, I'd synchronize to their movements. "Last night, around ten or so, Frank was saying he had to head back home. Said he got a call for a walk-on in one of the NCIS's, and had to go."

"Did he?" I asked.

Lewis shrugged while Roy kept looking down at the floor. "He didn't say anything about the part till yesterday. Carson said no problem, and to make sure he got home in time said he'd drive him out to the airport himself."

"That's how you guys came?" I asked. "By plane?"

They nodded in concert again.

"When'd you show up?" I asked.

"We've been here about a week," Lewis said.

Clearly, Carson had more of a mind for organization than I'd given him credit for.

"So Frank packed his bags and Carson and he took off," I said. "That's it."

"And a few hours later Carson came back by himself."

A couple beats of silence ticked by as the two young men absorbed that.

"Oh, shit," Lewis finally said.

"Why exactly did Carson bring you guys out here? What form did this dry run of yours take?"

"Mainly, he wanted to work out the logistics of how a bunch of hoods would operate in a small town like this. Where we would go, what we would do as we're tracking down this person trying to get to the feds."

It was becoming clear to me I hadn't given Carson enough credit. He seemed to have been working on a two-layered program, some actual tough guys he'd brought from California and this backup bunch of home-grown talent.

But I still couldn't quite see what the whole point of all these shenanigans were.

Including the fact I still didn't have a clue where Wendy Truell's three million dollars had gone to.

"He suckered us, didn't he?" Roy asked.

"Yeah," I said, "I'm afraid he did. You know where he is now?"

"Sure. When we left, he was still at the house we're renting."

"House?" I wanted to kick myself. It had never occurred to me to wonder where they'd been staying while in town.

"Yeah," Roy continued. "He rented a place about a week ago and got it all stocked up for us. It's not in such a great area, but the fridge is filled up and there's a 50-inch TV in each of our rooms so . . ." he trailed off and began looking a little sick.

I stood up, pulled my phone out, and dialed Nichols's number. "Let's go," I said, "you need to show me where that house is."

CHAPTER FORTY-EIGHT

I T WAS A LITTLE AFTER ELEVEN when I pulled up half a block down from a decent-sized house in one of our better neighborhoods. Not one of the areas where half a million-dollar houses are being constructed every day, to be filled with upwardly-mobile executives, doctors, and other professionals welcoming perpetual debt due to their mortgages, but a nice, slightly upper-middle class area, one of the original neighborhoods of Providence back in the old days.

A single-story house, made mainly of brick as far as I could tell in the dark, with enough trees in front to mask most of the home.

The guys were nervous, naturally. Roy sat next to me in the front seat, allowing me to clearly see him jittering a bit. I glanced in the rearview mirror. Lewis was hunched down, as if trying to be invisible from the world.

"So what's his plan?" I asked the guys.

"Well, see, that's just it," Roy said. "The last day or so, it's like he doesn't have much of a plan. You know those old-time pinball machines, where the ball bounces and zooms all over the place? That's how John's been."

"Has he stayed inside much?" I asked.

Roy waggled his hand. "Off and on. When he goes out, he borrows Lewis's old Dodge."

Which explained why the cops hadn't pinged on the Corvette

"There's a red Dodge parked at the curb," I said.

Lewis nodded in the seat behind me. "Yep, that's mine."

"Which means he's probably in there," I said.

Neither of the two guys responded to that. I pulled out my phone and placed a call to Nichols.

The good sergeant answered with a mumbly, just-went-to-sleep voice. "What's up?"

"Wakey, wakey, Josh," I said. "I think I've found your guy for you."

CHAPTER FORTY-NINE

LESS THAN A QUARTER HOUR AFTER I made the call, the cops began showing up. You had to look close for them, but two or three cars, with lights off, coasted into the darkened street. I assumed others lurked on the side streets and probably someone staking out the rear of the house.

The two actors and I stayed in my car. While I would only be in the way mixing in with the action, it had been a long week for me, and I wanted to be in on the end of it.

A few minutes later, my phone buzzed.

"Okay," Nichols said, "we're in position. You planning on hanging around?"

"If you don't mind. I won't get in the way."

"Damned right you won't. Both Santiago and Hendricks would have a fit if you did."

"Hendricks here too?" I asked.

"He's with me. Parked about three houses away from you."

"Straight up the drive?" I asked.

"Yep. This isn't a SWAT operation or anything. You sure he's still in there?"

"Far as we can tell, judging by the cars."

"Do your boys there know anything about the money?" he asked.

"I didn't ask them," I said. "My best guess at the moment is that the money's a sort of red herring."

"You mean a confusion factor to throw the blame onto others?" Nichols asked.

"Way I see it," I said.

"Okay, then. Lean back, break out your popcorn, and let's see what happens."

Nichols rang off, and I settled back in my seat. Lewis and Roy gave me questioning looks.

"Couple of minutes, guys, and it should be over with."

They didn't look all that reassured.

"Was he really going to be making a movie?" Lewis asked.

I worked my shoulders to get some kinks out. Maybe when this was all wrapped, I needed to get back to Keri Eckland's yoga. "You guys have to understand something. Mr. Carson in there doesn't exactly live in the real world. He probably thought he was going to make a movie or something, someday, but it was all really a way to con you and the others into working for him."

"The other guys are dead, aren't they?" Roy asked. "The others he brought from out west?"

"Most of them. One's in jail. But don't feel too bad. They were more legitimately harder guys."

Before I could say anymore. I heard the slightest double thunk of car doors closing, and a moment later two pairs of shadowy figures were approaching the house in question, one pair on each side.

I figured at least one or two other groupings of cops somewhere out front, maybe a little farther down the street, ready to zoom in if needed.

The four up front stood on the front porch for a moment, then went in. No one answered their knock, if in fact they did knock. They entered on their own.

I had to force myself to hold my breath as a moment later a light flicked on inside the house.

Another minute or two went by, and one by one more lights, both in front and to the sides, came on.

Then the porch light came on, and in a moment plainclothes cops from up and down the street flocked to the house.

"Dammit," I said.

"What?" Roy asked me.

I didn't know for sure, but I had a hunch. "He's not here."

Ten seconds later, the hunch blossomed as my cell phone buzzed.

"Yeah?" I said into the phone.

"He's not here," Nichols said.

"I'm not going to say something stupid like are you sure," I said. "But both cars are still here."

"Maybe he's heard of Uber," Nichols replied.

"Gone for good?" I asked.

"Looks like some of his stuff's been packed, but it's hard to tell. How many guys were living here?"

I looked over at Roy. "At least three."

"Yeah, well, if you've got two of them in your car better go ahead and bring them in."

"In the house?" I asked.

"Naw. Still won't hurt us to get crime scene out here. Bring them up to the front porch. We have some things to discuss with those young men."

CHAPTER FIFTY

"**G**LAD YOU CHECK YOUR MESSAGES," BERNIE Lyman said.
It was Sunday afternoon. After turning over Carson's playmates to the cops for further questioning, I'd gotten home around three in the morning.

I woke up about nine or so, had a quick breakfast, called Talia to get her up to speed on what had happened, then checked for other messages.

There was only the one from Bernie.

"What's up?"

"You may have lined up more work for me than you thought."

"Oh yeah?"

"My newest client called about three hours ago," Bernie said.

"Carson?" I asked.

"Yeah, or Lemwitz or whatever the hell his name is this week."

"He called you," I said.

"Yep. Told me he was leaving town but wanted to make sure I was available if he ever needed me again."

"Then he's definitely on the run," I said. Not even thinking of turning himself in?"

"Tell me, Sam, does this guy ever access any, you know, news?"

"How the hell would I know, Bernie? I barely know the guy. What time I've spent with him would incline me to think the only news he watches, reads, or hears is the entertainment stuff."

"Whatever," Bernie snorted, and I had to smile. In his own way,

Bernie was as narrowly focused in life as John Carson. Trying and winning cases was pretty much all he cared about, and the rest of life could go jump as far as he was concerned. "Your point is valid. I'd already gotten the rundown from Nichols, and suggested to Carson he turn himself in."

"How'd that go?" I asked.

"He was shocked, shocked he tells me. How could anyone possibly think he could do such a thing as kill his partner?"

"Which means he's decided not to turn himself in."

"Exactly that," Bernie said. "At which point I told him I could no longer represent him."

"Did he tell you to send him a bill?"

A half snort/ half laugh came over the phone. "Actually, he called me a crooked shyster and hung up on me."

"Shyster?" I said.

"A term I'm guessing he got from watching old movies. He doesn't seem to have a single original thought in his head, does he?"

"I wouldn't be too sure of that," I said. "I'm starting to think he was a lot more creative than I thought. You relay this info to Nichols?"

"I did, and he thanked me. If we're lucky, he's gone far away from here by now."

"I don't know," I said. "Once Hendricks gets in touch with his counterparts out in California, which he probably already has, I'm not sure there's any place ole' Johnny can run to. The feds are going to pounce on every inch of his life. And there's the issue of the supposed several million dollars still up in the air."

"Nichols shared with me your theory on that," Bernie said.

"Yeah. I think that was just a lot of misdirection. It's not all that hard to start a rumor in show business, you know."

"Well, for what it's worth, there's one more thing."

"Uh huh." I was almost fearful to hear what.

"I made a few calls to friends back west," Bernie said.

"Yeah?"

"Turns out your Monumental Productions has been catching people's interest for a while."

"What kind of people?"

"Accountants, tax folks, like that."

"Not unexpected," I said. "After all, Truell was running a money-launder through it, meaning things would naturally look a little hinky. Carson already explained to me they'd been running for almost a decade without showing a profit."

"Then he only told you half of it," Bernie said. "Maybe because he only knew the half."

"What's the other half?"

"According to people I talked to, and these are people who would know, not only were they running at a loss, they were running at a deliberate loss."

I frowned, not sure I'd heard him right. "What do you mean, deliberate loss?"

"I mean the company was already under the gun with financial investigators before all this began. Probably a major motivator for the Truell woman to offer herself up to the feds in the first place. Turns out when you really look close at the books, she was making deliberate decisions to lose money. For instance, if she had a choice between two vendors for a particular product or service, with all the factors being the same except cost, she'd invariably go with the one that cost more."

Took me a minute to spin that one around. "You saying she wanted to have their company in the red?"

"That's what I'm saying. According to my contacts, primarily someone in the tax business, there's no other explanation for it."

"Sounds like a nice little front she had going," I said.

"It was. Except there's always other people involved, and sooner or later someone's going to come around asking questions."

"And about the time the questions began piling up," I said, "she decided she'd had a nice run and it was time to offer herself up to the government."

"That's the way it reads for most of the people looking into it," Bernie said.

"And if somehow Carson got wind of her plans, he saw his gravy train coming to an end."

"The other way to look at it, though," Bernie said. "Is this really our problem anymore?"

"Doesn't seem to be," I said.

CHAPTER FIFTY-ONE

THE NEXT CALL, ABOUT TEN MINUTES later, came from Josh Nichols.

"Your boy's in the wind for sure. We're looking everywhere, including the room at the Radisson that he never checked out of, and he hasn't shown yet."

"What's Hendricks say?" I asked.

"If I were you, buddy, I'd steer clear of any federal buildings for a while."

"Not that hard to do around here," I said.

"Yeah, but believe me, your favorite fed was in here chewing nails not all that long ago. He was yelling loud enough in Santiago's office it rattled windows in the parking garage."

"Your parking garage doesn't have windows," I pointed out.

"Gives you an idea of how loud he was yelling."

"Santiago back at work all the way?" I asked.

"Yep, and from what I gather he's about the only thing preventing the feds from sweeping down on you. You know how they hate to be embarrassed."

"You point out I was the one who gave the tip of where he'd been staying?"

"Santiago did, but it didn't seem to mollify Hendricks in the least. Said if we hadn't had amateurs mucking around in this, it wouldn't have gotten this far out of hand."

"Guess I'll scratch him off my fan club mailing list," I said.

"I'd do more than that were I you, buddy. I'm serious Sam, don't even drive by the downtown post office for a while. You never saw someone so bent out of shape."

"Can't say as I blame him," I said. "They had an absolute golden goose ready to go in Wendy Truell, and it blew up in their faces."

"True. But you weren't the guy who set it off. And the lieutenant took great pains to explain that to Hendricks."

"Santiago stood up for me?" Despite my image as a tough guy, I couldn't help my voice squeaking in surprise.

"Do me a favor, Blondie. Don't tell him I said that or I'll be busted down to animal control or some such."

"Safe with me," I said. "Still leaves us the problem of tracking down Carson. We're both pretty sure he's a double murderer, at the very least."

"This is true."

"You find any trace of the money?" I asked.

"The mythical three million dollars we keep hearing about but never see a trace of?"

"Yeah," I said, "that money."

"Nope. Neither hide nor hair. I'm guessing the same as you. The three million probably never existed as such. You managed to track him down when we couldn't. You happen to have any other bright ideas?"

I slumped in my seat, suddenly exhausted with the whole damned thing. "Not right now, but if I think of any you'll be the first to know."

"Works for me," Nichols said, and we disconnected.

I didn't know what to do. I could go out and drive around town looking for my wayward client, but the cops were already doing that. I could take a flight out to the east coast and solve the Jimmy Hoffa disappearance, but even that probably wouldn't put me on Hendricks's good side.

It occurred to me I should have steered Bernie Lyman to Lewis and Roy, seeing as how I doubted two twenty-something acting students knew much in the way of legal representation in Missouri, but I found I didn't really give a damn what happened to those two.

I thought of calling Talia and seeing if she wanted to spend the day together but knew I was in too sour of a mood to be much fun.

Maybe if I spent enough time staring at the walls of my apartment, something would come to me.

Maybe, but probably not.

CHAPTER FIFTY-TWO

I SPENT MONDAY AS A FAIRLY NORMAL day. Did some work in my office at the gym, worked out a bit in the afternoon, and kept in touch with Nichols as the manhunt for John Carson continued. So far, no sign of him.

I went out for dinner and some drinks, arriving home a little after ten. I had a female friend with me who wasn't Talia Sanderson. We'd eaten at a local steak house, not one of the chains which dot Arena Avenue but one a little off the beaten path, then stopped off at a couple of bars for drinks and some music.

Talia thought I was working late at The Blaster, giving both Lisa and Keri a night off.

We both acted a little tipsy as we got to my apartment door. I fumbled a bit till I got the right key, managed to slide it into my lock in one go, then twisted the knob at the same time my friend, a fairly tall black woman, wrapped her arms around me.

I had to work to hold her up as she was really bending at the knees.

We half tumbled, half stumbled into my living room, and because we were preoccupied with staying upright we at first didn't notice the shadow that split off from a corner of the hall and came up behind us.

Something round and hard, something I identified from experience, shoved into my back.

"Move on in, Blondie, and shut the door."

As we stumbled in, John Carson behind us, my friend half turned away, as if ashamed to be seen by anyone.

In the sudden rush of movement, her purse got knocked out of her hand and spilled open onto the floor. She left it there, no doubt thinking, as I did, this strange man with a weapon drawn on us took precedence over a spilled purse.

A moment later, completely sober, I stood a little straighter. "What are you doing here, John?"

Carson shut and locked the door, moved away from us, and sat down in one of my chairs.

He looked more disheveled than I think I've ever seen anyone outside of a bar. He didn't appear drunk but had the wild look, the red eyes and rumpled clothing, of a man who'd been moving constantly for days on end.

The gun never wavered in his grip.

"Can you tell me any place I should be? The cops and feds are looking for me."

"So?"

"So I can't go back to the hotel 'cause they've probably got it staked out. Obviously can't go back to that house I was staying with those two posers since the cops busted in."

"You could have left town," I said.

Carson snickered. "You think I didn't think of something that obvious? The problem is, thanks to you, the feds are looking for me as well. Dodging your locals isn't any big deal, but the F.B.I is something else."

"Then what do you want out of me?" I said. So far, my friend hadn't said anything but had stayed huddled against the door.

"I want you to know how much you screwed me up," Carson said. "Once I got Wendy out of the picture, I was in position to take Monumental over completely and go on with business as usual. *All* business as usual. You know what kind of wheel I could have been with all that money backing me up?"

"I thought I was getting you out of a jam."

"Well, doesn't matter. It's blown now. If I go back, even if I do evade the feds, you think the boys will want to go into business with me?"

I looked closely at the automatic he held. As far as I could tell, it was the real thing, not a prop gun or anything like that. I had to assume even a doofus like John Carson would have the thing actually loaded.

"Hey," he suddenly said. "Who's the girl?"

If anything, she turned more away from him than she had been.

"A friend," I said.

"It's not Dr. Sanderson."

"No, she's not. Just a friend."

Carson shook his head, then gestured with the automatic. "How about you and your friend go over and sit down."

The two of us walked to the couch, me partially shielding her. Carson kept his eyes on us the whole time.

I tensed up in case he gave me an opening to make a move and did my best to keep the woman between me and him.

We sat down. I sat closest to Carson, hoping to keep some distance between him the woman.

The three of us looked at each other.

"Who's your friend, Sam?"

She slouched even further down. "Her name's Julie," I said.

"Sorry about this, Julie. I expected him to be coming home alone."

"Well," I said, "what's your plan John?"

"Not sure. You really kind of screwed me over, Sam."

"Not the way I see it," I said. "You did kill Wendy, right?"

"What if I did?"

"If you did, I'd guess it was your plan all along. Even before you came out here."

He cracked a grin, though one that looked a little pained. "Looks like you're not as dumb as I thought you were, Sam. Sure, I had it all worked out."

Julie's eyes widened at that.

"Including the hoods from out of state? A bunch of lower-level goons and some bit-part actors who thought you were giving them the chance of a lifetime?"

Carson shook his head again. "You figured that out as well?"

"Wasn't hard, especially once we backtracked Frank Weatherly. You kill him too?"

Carson tensed up. "I think we've talked about this enough, Sam."

"Then what are we going to do, John? Sit around glaring at each other all night till we fall asleep? Julie here has to go to work in the morning."

"I need to make sure you don't talk."

"Yeah?"

"But I'm not too sure how to do that," Carson said.

I realized then he was playing things by ear and not doing a very good job of it.

"You're a lousy booker, John," I said.

"A what?"

"Sorry," I said as Julie brushed her hand against my thigh. "Phrase from my previous life. A booker is the guy who plots out the matches. Who fights against whom, who wins, any particular high spots to have in the match, and anything that happens after."

Carson frowned. "You mean like it's all written out ahead of time?"

"Not all of it, but the main beats, more or less. And the guy who does it is called the booker."

"So your wrestling is really nothing more than another type of scripted show?" Carson asked.

I thought about it for a moment, then nodded. "I guess so, never quite thought of it that way, but yeah."

"So why do you say I'm not a good one?" Carson asked.

"Because you didn't plan for alterations in the book. You thought you'd shanghai out here with Wendy, out where nobody knows you and away from the bright lights, and bump her off. You even hired some people and brought them out to make everyone think for sure it was some of her mob friends who did her in. How am I doing?"

Carson's eyes narrowed. "I'm starting to think you may be wearing a wire, Sam."

I shook my head. "Come on, man. That's more bad TV. Nobody

has to wear wires anymore. All anyone has to do is tap their cell phone and you're recording."

"Wouldn't do you any good, Sam. For it to be entered as evidence, both parties have to consent. And I say no."

I shook my head. "That's what I meant by not being good at this, John. You're thinking of California. Out here, we're a one-party state. As long as one person consents to being recorded, the evidence stands up."

I should know, after all. Just a couple of days before I'd pulled a similar trick on Mark Farrell to get Santiago off the hook.

Carson's eyes slitted even more. "Take out your phone, Sam."

"Huh?"

"Take your phone out of your pocket and toss it on the floor over there." With the gun, he pointed at a spot about six feet away from him.

"Not a chance," I said.

Carson moved the position of his weapon slightly. "Do it, or I put one through your sleepy friend there."

Even as loose as she was, I felt Julie tense beside me. I looked closely at John and could tell that, at least for the moment, he meant business.

I pulled my phone out of my rear pocket and tossed it over where he'd indicated.

Carson got up from his chair and walked over without ever veering in the general direction of the gun. When he got to my phone, he raised his right foot and stomped it down, grinding the splintered remains into the carpet.

Without turning his back, he walked back over and sat back down in the chair.

For a moment, he stared at Julie lolling against me.

"Got to say, guy," he said, "I'm a little disappointed in you. Dr. Sanderson seemed like a classy woman. This one looks pretty much a tramp."

"What are you going to do, John? How's this going to play out?"

"What would you do? How would you—what did you call it—book the way this ends?"

"How about with giving me the gun?" I suggested.

Carson chuckled. "You kidding? I've got Monumental Productions, now. It's all mine. I've got Wendy's contacts who still need a place to wash their funds. All I have to do is take care of you, and your friend there, and I'm home clean."

"Aren't you forgetting the cops? The feds? If they weren't a problem, you would have already been on a plane back to L.A. by now."

He frowned, and something kind of dark flickered across his face. "I should be. I would have been. The whole point was to set it up to have the cops chasing their tails all over the place looking for the cartel scum that killed Wendy."

"I got that," I said.

"But then you had to go and start nosing around in the wrong places. I'm guessing you're the one who figured out who all the gunmen after us really were?"

"I helped, but Nichols and his people would have figured it out themselves before too long."

"Thanks a lot, buddy."

"Then this is all my fault?" I asked.

"Damned straight. I had it all fixed: Wendy dead, some phantom gangsters to blame, and myself sitting pretty. You tell me, Blond Bomber. If you were me, how would you write the ending?"

"It depends."

"On?"

"On where the money is," I said. "What happened to the three million? Or did it even exist?"

Carson flinched, and a small tick developed over his right eye. "You got that too?"

I shrugged. "It makes the most sense. In the lingo of my old days, you overbooked. What'd you do? Plant the word around about the three million just to make up a motive for Wendy's murder?"

"I had to have some reason. I knew I'd be the most likely suspect, so I had to have something to get the cops looking somewhere else."

"Hell," I said, more to myself than him. "You didn't know she was going to enter the federal program, did you? You flat wanted her out of the way?"

Carson nodded, a pained look on his face. "Turns out I could have spared myself the trouble of planting a motive. Wendy had already done that, in real life."

"Damn, John," I said. "That really bites."

He waggled the gun at me. "Back to my question, Sam. If you were to—what'd you call it—book this, how would it end?"

"Maybe with some sorrow on your part," I said. "Was it really that easy to knock off your business partner of eight years?"

Something flickered across Carson's face, something beyond the fakeness I was used to seeing there. "You think it was easy?"

"That's what I'm asking," I said. "It mustn't have been any big deal, seeing as how it doesn't seem to have slowed you down any."

That something flickered again, a bit more intense this time. "Guess again, buddy. You're right in that I figured I'd just waltz into her suite, wait till she got there, and pump a couple into her."

"Didn't work out that way, did it?" I asked.

He shook his head, violently. As if trying to expel something from his memory. "It was hard. I got into her suite and waited, Then I came up behind her, but she must have heard something. She turned at the last minute and looked right at me. I could tell she was going to scream. I didn't know how much or whether it would carry out of the suite. I shot her straight on, with her looking at me. Not the way I wanted it to go at all."

I'd had about enough of looking down Carson's gun barrel. I turned to Julie. "You heard enough?"

She raised her head from my shoulder and nodded.

Carson blinked. He leaned forward, and his finger tightened on the trigger. I came off the couch in an almost horizontal motion and flung myself straight at him, still sitting in the leather chair.

It was a reckless move, but Julie had been holding her weapon in between her thighs ever since digging it from her purse back at the door, and I didn't know if she could get it up and leveled before Carson could shoot.

I figured he may be expecting a lot of things, but someone of well over two-hundred pounds flying straight at him wouldn't' be one of them.

After all, no one could be that stupid.

I crossed my arms in front of my chest as I flew, hitting him full on, chest to chest. Naturally, we tipped over in a three-layer pile on the floor: first the chair, then Carson, and then me.

With this, my back was turned to Julie, and I had no doubt she was probably really pissed at me about then. Out of the corner of my eye, I saw Carson's right arm had flung to the side as we crashed to the floor, and I brought the edge of my left hand down in as fierce a chop as I could.

His fingers splayed, the gun flopped out of them, and Julie rushed over and grabbed it in her left hand.

Her weapon was a small .22 caliber pistol. Not her regular service weapon, but when we'd headed out for the night, she'd opted for something that could be concealed easier.

To be on the safe side, I drove a pretty solid right hook into Carson's jaw, not enough to knock him out, but enough to keep him woozy for a few seconds until I could disentangle myself and stand up.

Julie tossed me the little .22 and kept Carson's automatic leveled at him.

"Not bad, Detective," I said.

"Thanks," Julie replied as Carson began to come out of it.

He made a few whupping and whooing sounds until his eyes unglazed by about half, and Julie motioned him to get up.

"You're under arrest, mister," she said.

"What?" Carson's focus still hadn't come back entirely, but he was clearing by the second.

"I guess I should introduce you guys," I said. "John Carson, soon to be former television producer, this is Detective Julie Francis of the Providence PD."

Detective Francis gave Carson a high-wattage smile.

"I want you to know," she said, "I really hate reality shows."

CHAPTER FIFTY-THREE

SHORTLY AFTER NINE THE NEXT MORNING, Santiago knocked on my office door. I had the door open, as I usually do, but he knocked anyway.

Unusual for the guy, who usually bulled in to wherever he wanted.

I waved him in. He went straight to the coffee maker in the corner and glanced my way. I nodded, and a moment later the two of us were relaxing, me behind my desk and the lieutenant in one of the other chairs, coffee cups in hand.

He was back in full Lt. Santiago mode. A light gray silk suit, dark blue French-cuff shirt, and solid scarlet tie. His black loafers were so polished I could see the overhead lights reflected in them.

"We processed Carson early this morning," he said after taking a sip from his cup.

"He get a lawyer?" I asked.

Santiago shook his head. "He tried to call Lyman, but Bernie did everything short of changing his phone number. He made a few calls out west but nothing came of them. He may have to go the public defender route, at least to start."

"My guess," I said, "is he's not exactly flush with ready cash."

"Who knows?" Santiago said. "Actually, who really cares? He's not going anywhere for a long time. But there's one thing I still don't get."

"What's that?" I asked.

"The whole kidnapping thing, including the disposable phone. What the hell was that about?"

I leaned as far back as I could and stared at the ceiling for a minute.

"The same as the phantom three million dollars," I finally said. "More overbooking on his part. He had one of those kids make the call. Throwing everything he could into the mix, probably hoping like hell it would keep attention diverted away from him and onto those make-believe gangsters of his."

"Makes sense, kind of," Santiago said.

"Then again, maybe it's just part of his overdramatic flakiness."

We drank silently for a few minutes. I knew the lieutenant hadn't come all the way over just to deliver news he could have over the phone. Far as that went, he didn't have to deliver it at all, seeing as my part in the whole John Carson affair was pretty much wrapped.

After that short pause, though, Santiago spoke up.

"I joined the force in Chicago the day I turned twenty-one," he said, looking at the wall more than at me.

I stayed quiet and waited for him to continue.

"The force had an unwritten policy back then, hell maybe they still have it, that as many newbies as possible would be assigned to the worst precincts in the city. Like, okay, you've made it through the academy, but here's one last test. See if you can cut it."

"Kind of like making doctors in residency work hundred-hour weeks," I said.

Santiago nodded. "I don't think hospitals do that anymore, but yeah, that's the basic idea. Kind of short-sighted if you think of it. They ended up putting me in the worst of the worst."

We both paused for another drink before he continued.

"About a year into my term in that shithole, a young public defender was assigned to our precinct. Name was Rachel Stinton."

He looked at me for a moment. I shook my head to show my confusion.

"Her old man was Harry 'Call Me Hal' Stinton. If you had a personal injury suit anywhere within fifty miles of Cook County, and you got a ridiculously large settlement, odds were Stinton was your lawyer."

"His daughter didn't share his pragmatic approach to the law?" I asked.

Santiago held his hand up and wiggled it back and forth. "Let's say she felt the need to help the unfortunate in a different way than her father did."

I finished my coffee, crumpled the cup, and tossed it into the wastebasket by my desk. "Sounds like you knew her pretty well," I said.

Santiago's face set a little, becoming a little stonier than usual. "Young cop in uniform, ready to take down all the bad guys? Idealistic young PD wanting to let them all go free? Yeah, we got to know each other."

I had a hunch where this was all leading, but I also knew the lieutenant had to get there on his own.

"What the hell," he said. "No real reason to be coy. Yeah, we started seeing each other. As the weeks and months went on, it got more and more serious."

"How serious?" I asked.

He looked away from me for a moment, staring at the wall to his left. "We got engaged," he finally said. "And right after, I put in for a transfer."

Okay, I hadn't seen that one coming.

"It was the only practical thing to do," Santiago continued. "I know this will sound egotistical as hell, but I was on a rocket ship career wise. Only a couple of years on the force and I was already being talked about to move up to sergeant. Rachel and I talked it over, and we decided there would be too much room for gossip and misinformation if we stayed in the same precinct."

"You asking for a transfer didn't hurt your promotion chances?" I asked.

Santiago shook his head. "If anything, it helped. Everyone knew about me and Rachel, meaning I was seen as doing the proper thing to eliminate any conflict of interest. The sergeant's exam was coming up, and my former squad commander made a point of getting me on the list for the test."

"Okay."

Santiago got up and made himself another cup of coffee. He glanced my way, but I shook my head.

"So anyway," he said as he sat back down, "we had everything out of the way and cleared up. Once my transfer was official, we set a date and got hitched. I settled down to live happily ever after."

He frowned, and his eyes hooded over. I had a feeling we were getting to whatever the point was.

Though I wasn't all too sure I wanted to get there with him.

"Because of my transfer," he said, "I wasn't in the old precinct house a few months later when one of the squad did a poor job of frisking an assault suspect. While he was consulting with his attorney, the collar pulled out a knife and cut her up."

"The attorney being Rachel," I said.

Santiago nodded, his eyes still hooded.

I had time to take several deep breaths before he continued.

"People at the hospital did their best, but she was too cut up. She died on the table about six hours later."

"I'm sorry," I said.

He nodded and blinked a couple of times. I thought I saw his eyes glisten a little, but I wasn't sure.

"As you can probably imagine, Hal Stinson was damned near devasted."

"Couldn't have been any too easy for you," I pointed out.

"True. For a long time, all I wanted to do was get my hands on the cop who'd pulled such a rookie mistake. Can you imagine not doing a full pat-down on an arrestee? Especially before isolating him in a room with a young female attorney? A lot of people kept an eye on me for a long time to make sure I didn't go after the fuckup."

"That wasn't the end of things, was it?" I asked.

Santiago shook his head. "Rachel's old man was almost catatonic after losing her, but his partners weren't. They went after the city big time."

"That put you in anybody's crosshairs?"

Santiago finished his coffee, then duplicated my feat of crumpling his cup and tossing it in the trash.

Since the cups were Styrofoam and the basket was a couple of feet away, not a great feat. But guys have to match each other no matter what.

"You'd think so, but again, all things considered the brass were pretty good about it. Especially since I made clear from the get go, to whoever would listen, I wasn't taking part in any settlement."

"Really?"

The lieutenant took a deep breath. "You've got to understand, Quinton, all I ever wanted to be was a cop. First, last, and always. Going in, I knew about the pay, the conditions, and all of that. Didn't matter, being a cop through and through was all I wanted."

"And if you took any money from the settlement for your wife's death . . ."

"It could have damaged my relationships in the department. Maybe not publicly, not overtly. But damaged."

"Was there a settlement?" I asked.

"Uh huh."

"How much?"

"Trust me, you don't want to know. My father-in-law and his partners offered to split with me, and like I'd already said, I turned them down."

"And went on being a cop," I said.

"Yeah."

Something in his tone, something about the expression on his face, said there was more. "But?"

"But my turning the money down didn't matter. People started looking sideways at me, and I heard the occasional whisper behind my back. I worked harder than ever, harder than anyone else, until I eventually made lieutenant."

"Didn't stop the whispers, did it?" I asked.

"Nope. But shortly after something happened that made me not give a damn about them."

Out of the blue, I found myself holding my breath. Something was coming up, something big, but Santiago had to get to it in his own way.

"A couple of years after Rachel's killing, and a few months after I made lieutenant grade, Hal Stinson passed away."

"Accident of some kind?" I asked.

"Nope. Pancreatic cancer. Came on him quick, killed him even quicker. Rachel was his only kid, there were no grandkids and I guess after her killing not much of a reason to keep on going."

"That's tough, Bill."

Santiago nodded. He took a deep breath, sat up straighter in his chair. I had a feeling we were getting to it. "I was asked to come to the reading of his will. When I got the summons, I assumed he'd left me something, you know, considering my marriage to Rachel."

"Makes sense."

"He left me his share of the settlement money," he said, his voice almost a whisper.

I blinked a couple of times. "How much did he have left?"

"Enough. He hardly spent any of it. I think he'd been more interested in getting the city's attention than anything. And there weren't any other kids, and Rachel's mom had died years ago. Hal kept it all in interest-bearing accounts with instructions it was to go to me upon his death. His partners, who pushed the original suit, of course took their cut. But even there, I got the feeling they didn't take much ."

"And he gave it all to you," I said. "Jesus Christ."

"Yeah," Santiago said. "Pretty much."

"But you kept on working? How much are we talking? Somewhere in the six figures?"

Santiago grinned, the first light emotion he'd shown since entering my office. "Add another zero, and you'll be in the ballpark."

I shook my head, feeling as if my brain was flying apart. It had always been obvious Santiago had extra funds from somewhere, but until right then I'd never quite had a handle on how much.

"At first I was going to give it away," he continued. "Find a couple of decent charities and make them a gift. But then I got to thinking."

"Yeah?"

"Yeah. All I'd ever wanted to be was cop and with all the extra dough, I could be the best possible kind of cop I could."

I had to roll that around in the head for a few minutes before what he meant popped out the other end. "Because you couldn't be corrupted."

Santiago nodded. "No matter what the wise guys would throw at me, it wouldn't matter because I'd know in my heart that, no matter what, there wasn't anything they could give me I couldn't get on my own if I wanted it."

"What about other cops suspecting you of something?" I asked.

Santiago shrugged. "Bothered me, sure. But the important thing was for me to know I couldn't be bought."

"True," I said, "but it does lead to another possible problem."

"Which would be?"

I waved my hand in his direction. "Your lifestyle. You're kind of making it obvious you've got something on the ball somewhere."

He grinned. "That's right. But anyone who would be tempted to make a run at me assumes I'm in someone else's pocket. Even so, a lot of them couldn't resist the challenge and came sniffing around me, which helped us close a lot of cases."

Now it was my turn to nod. "And since they don't know for sure whose . . ."

"They all give me a wide berth."

I could still see one flaw in his thinking. "But it does make you a target for doofusses like Mark Farrell."

Santiago stood up. "Then I guess it's a good thing I have some people I can trust to watch my back, huh?"

"Can't hurt," I said.

"As for our old buddy Councilman Farrell, the district attorney's office has been having quite a good time going over that tape of yours. From what I gather, a couple of phone calls have been made, and if Farrell's smart he'd better get set for a whole lot of legal hell, up to and including the IRS, to come crashing down on him."

"What about the DEA?" I asked.

Santiago grinned. "You mean are they the least bit interested in a major pipeline of almost pure stuff coming through the mid-section of the country? Of course, they are." He took a moment to glance at his watch. Omega, of course. "The hotel's should be filling up right about now."

"Should keep the councilman busy enough with his own problems that he doesn't have time to come after you anymore."

Santiago's grin sobered a bit. "I think we can be assured of that."

"Pleasure doing business with you," I said.

The lieutenant held his hand up in the shape of a gun, cocked his thumb, and pulled the trigger finger.

He was half out the door when I spoke up. "One other thing."

He turned back. "Yeah?"

"The other day when I was talking to Lou Di Maglia."

"What about it?"

"He implied some sort of connection with you. If you're so above it all, what's the deal there?"

Santiago smiled. "Story for another day, Quinton."

And he walked out.

I sat there thinking for a few minutes, didn't reach any particular conclusion, and heaved myself up from behind my desk.

Time to do some regular work for a change.

Especially now that my one and only Hollywood connection had pretty much fizzled out.

A RETIRED HIGH-SCHOOL TEACHER AND FORMER COLLEGE instructor, Kevin R. Doyle is the author of six novels in the Sam Quinton mystery series, all published by Camel Press. He's also written four crime thrillers, including *And the Devil Walks Away* and *The Anchor*, and one horror novel, *The Litter*, along with numerous short horror stories published in small magazines over the years. The first Quinton book, *Squatter's Rights*, was shortlisted for the 2021 Shamus award for Best First PI Novel.

www.ingramcontent.com/pod-product-compliance
Lightning Source LLC
Chambersburg PA
CBHW011515100726
47899CB00010BD/3370